A Web

To my Momma Jay!

Love,

[signature]

A Web of Truth

Sonya Carlan

TATE PUBLISHING
AND ENTERPRISES, LLC

The opinions expressed by the author are not necessarily those of Tate Publishing, LLC.

Published by Tate Publishing & Enterprises, LLC
127 E. Trade Center Terrace | Mustang, Oklahoma 73064 USA
1.888.361.9473 | www.tatepublishing.com

Tate Publishing is committed to excellence in the publishing industry. The company reflects the philosophy established by the founders, based on Psalm 68:11,
"The Lord gave the word and great was the company of those who published it."

Book design copyright © 2014 by Tate Publishing, LLC. All rights reserved.

Published in the United States of America

ISBN: 978-1-63185-232-9
1. Fiction/Christian/ General
2. Fiction/Christian/Romance
14.01.23

Chapter 1

The breeze blowing through her dark brown hair felt good on such a hot and sticky day. The heat was like a warm blanket around her shoulders and the sunshine lightly kissed her high cheek bones. She always enjoyed working in the garden with the other children. There were usually about ten or more kids at the house, including her. It didn't even matter that she wasn't out on her bike or climbing a tree. This was as fun as any game they ever played. She felt like she belonged; like she made a difference in someone's life. She had a family, siblings, people who cared for her as more than just an obligation. She had people who loved her unconditionally. If only it could always be this way. If only she could stay here forever, never go back. So many good times....

Bang! Bang! Bang! A loud knock on her office door jolted Darcy Scott out of her reverie. Bang! Bang! There it goes again. Who in the world is banging so hard on the door, she wondered. Irritation immediately flared up as she ran her hands through her hair. How many times had she told people that if her door was closed, she was busy? That was code for Go Away! Obviously she was going to have to get a sign that said just that.

"I'm coming. Just a minute," she yelled as she pushed her chair away from her intimidatingly large oak desk. Wow her legs were stiff. How long had she been sitting here today just dreaming?

It seemed she had been taking frequent trips down memory lane these days, much more than usual. Zoning out, as her boyfriend Michael liked to call it. Lahlah Land, maybe. No matter what you called it, it was nice. It always left her feeling warm all over, except of course when someone decided to be rude and interrupt her visit to Lahlah Land. That happened more than she liked to admit. Her fantasy trips were always to the same place, over and over again. She knew she really couldn't be mad at whoever was so impatient to get through her door because this just happened to be the worst time ever to be daydreaming with her work being so demanding and her personal life breathing down her throat. A break must be in her destiny.

"Maybe I've got ADD," Darcy thought with a chuckle as she reached for the door knob.

There just never seemed to be enough hours in a day, or at least in any of the days that Darcy seemed to exist in. If it got any more hectic, her plants were probably going to wilt and die from neglect. Maybe she should trade them all for a large cactus or any plant that was drought resistant. She was regularly aware of why she did not own a pet. The poor animal would go unnoticed for long amounts of time and possibly starve. Scatter brained, she was. Unfortunately she just couldn't seem to help it lately. It was as if her mind were taking road trips completely on its own. The past haunted her waking hours now more than ever. If something didn't change there might definitely be a nice white jacket in her future as well as a large bald orderly to clasp it in the back.

Darcy had no shortage of issues to plague her thoughts. Lucky her. Most of her painful memories came from being raised in a troubled household.

Her mother was a sloppy, rude alcoholic and she treated Darcy as if she were a burden just by existing. It was as if the child should have known better than to come into this world and ruin her mother's perfectly good day. The real burden was really Darcy's because she had to smell her mother each night when she finally came stumbling in from God knows where.

Where was the little girl's father you ask? That's a great question. It was a question that she herself had wondered a few times in her life.

Her father was simply absent, nothing more. She couldn't even remember what he looked like. This may have been a blessing since the other parent she had wasn't that great of an example. It didn't help that her mother had no pictures of the man. Maybe he was never meant to exist, at least not to Darcy. Some days she simply wondered what possessed her mother to even stick around considering she obviously had no interest in doing the 'parent thing.' Some people just aren't cut out for children of their own. Some people never stop being just big selfish children themselves.

Darcy used to think that her mother didn't like her because she had always been skinny with knobby knees and crooked teeth. She never seemed to measure up to those little girls you saw in the department store with their moms, all golden flowing hair, and pretty little Mary Janes to match their pressed and perfect little dresses. Darcy just wasn't that kind of kid. Too often her knees were covered in scabs from acting like a boy and she usually kept a foreign substance stuck in her short cropped hair. It didn't take long for her to realize it had nothing to do with her appearance. It was all about the drink for her mother. Alcohol ranked number one priority in her mom's life, never her daughter.

Chapter 2

There had come a time when Darcy was six years old that the state felt her mother, Marsha Scott, was unable to properly care for her daughter. A concerned neighbor was most likely the informant. They had no family around. It could have even been the hot dog vendor who always smiled at her when she walked home, most times alone. She saw the looks of pity that people gave her. So when the authorities showed up at the doorstep early one morning, it wasn't really a surprise. Marsha put up an ugly scene when the social worker came inside to physically remove her daughter. It really was an Oscar winning performance. Marsha probably told all her low rent friends at the bar how she told that social worker 'a thing or two."

She didn't really want Darcy, that was obvious, but pride overtook common sense and she refused to lie down quietly while the state took what she deemed as 'her property.' In the end, no matter how loud Marsha got, Darcy was taken away. She was removed from her mother's custody and placed in a foster home.

As bad as life at home was, she was terrified to be taken from the only parent she had ever known. The unknown could often be worse to a lonely child. Every horrible thought a kid could think went through her mind that day as she rode in back of the small white van heading to a destination unknown. She shed hundreds of tears on the ride to her new temporary home.

What if these people were angry that they had to care for another kid with no parent?

What if they didn't like her either?

Where would she go next?

The little girl knew her mother considered her an inconvenience and she was afraid her mother would never come for her again. The van bounced down a long dirt drive after being on the road for what seemed like an eternity. The sprawling countryside seemed to go on forever with nothing but fields in sight until suddenly she could see a gate. The driver drove through the gate as if he had done it literally a thousand times. When the house finally came into sight it looked as if the yard was growing kids of all ages. Darcy had never been with kids her own age except for schooling. She had no siblings, no cousins, and no neighbor friends to play with. The idea suddenly frightened her more than coming here alone. Being dropped off with strangers is bad enough but now she had more kids who might not like her. It didn't take long to see that it was nothing like she expected. All the fear that had built up in her little mind was quickly dispelled.

Chapter 3

Even at the age of twenty-six Darcy still had fond memories of the family that she had spent over two years with. Two years would be the amount of time that she would make their house her home and the people inside, her family. Albert and Kim Boyden owned the home and had two boys of their own, Davis and Jonah, not counting the many other children like Darcy. The Boydens were an emergency care foster family.

New children were constantly arriving at all hours of the night and day. Some stayed just the night, others stayed longer, as did Darcy. No matter how long they stayed, they were made to feel like they belonged in that home more than anyone else.

Mrs. Boyden was the first to greet Darcy and the social worker at the rear entrance to the house. She was a curvaceous little woman who wore her apron around her waist as if it was the only thing holding her together. She spoke softly to the woman who brought Darcy inside and wiped her flour dusted hands on her apron front.

After the particulars of signed paperwork and the exchange of information were taken care of, Darcy was given Mrs. Boyden's full attention.

The smile that Kim Boyden shown on Darcy was all it took to calm the shaking in her little hands. Nobody had ever smiled so brightly at the thought of being with Darcy. Why, her own mother looked at her with loathing every time she had to speak to the child. Why would a stranger be so happy to see her?

The social worker said her goodbyes and made sure to warn the child to "be good" and she would see them soon. Darcy was glad she was leaving. The social worker had a pinched face and smelled like wet cardboard. It made her very uncomfortable. This lady staring at her now wasn't like that at all. She was warm and soft and smelled like fresh bread. Darcy liked that a lot. Kim took Darcy's bag from her hand and squatted in front of her.

"We've been waiting for you dear. Don't be afraid. We're going to have a great time. I promise." She patted the child's shoulder softly and stood up.

Kim pulled a kitchen chair out for Darcy and sat the girl down in front of a plate of warm cookies and a small glass of milk. Suddenly a small smile spread out on Darcy's face. She had obviously died and gone to good kid heaven because this could not be real.

"Thank you ma'am. I like cookies," Darcy declared. She wiped her hair out of her small face and reached for a cookie. This was like living in luxury, she was sure nothing could be better.

The Boyden family lived on a sizable farm in Carter, Oklahoma in a modest two story beige clapboard house. The family wasn't rich by any means but they never turned anyone away. They always gave to anyone in need. The old saying, 'salt of the earth,' that was Albert and Kim. There were so many pleasant memories to recall about those days but the one special thing that always came back to Darcy was something that all the kids loved most.

There was a wooden play gym, the kind with the old tires to crawl through and the swinging bar, out in the yard. The special thing about this one was that it had a rope bridge attached to it that you could actually walk across to another wooden play gym.

The kids ran back and forth, back and forth on that old rope bridge for hours at a time. It was everyone's special place. If only Darcy could go back just once and sit on that old bridge she would be able to remember how happy she had been for a short time. Happy like she never thought she could be when she lived at home with the woman she called 'Mom.'

Chapter 4

It seemed that all Darcy could think about the past year was going back to that farm house and seeing those people again. Feeling just a little of that love again. However, going back now was almost impossible for several reasons.

Firstly, the amount of children who came through the doors of the Boyden household was huge and they probably would not even remember the sad little girl named Darcy Scott. Secondly, she was fifteen hundred miles away from that Oklahoma ranch. She was in New York where her mother had moved her once she was allowed to regain custody of her daughter. New York was a world away from Oklahoma in more ways than mileage.

The move was supposed to be a new start. A clean slate. Marsha had insisted that she had given up alcohol and had a great new job waiting on her among the hustle and bustle of the New York City streets. According to the Oklahoma State Protective Services, Marsha Scott had completed a series of drug and alcohol classes, hence proving her qualifications as a responsible parent. The social worker felt so confident with Marsha that they agreed to allow her to move her and her minor daughter out of state for a so-called 'new life.'

Darcy had never been secure with her mother but, as any eight-year old, she believed the best from the woman who gave her life. What other choice did she have? She was so excited that her mother was clean and sober. It was what the young girl had been praying for. The sad part was that Darcy had grown to love the Boyden family and thought of them as her parents. She thought of their home as her home. It was the longest time she had ever lived in one place. Her little heart was so torn between the family that loved her like she was their own and the mother that she wanted to love her. Being veteran foster parents, Albert and Kim knew when it was necessary to say goodbye to a child in their care. It did not make the sadness any less on the day that a social worker pulled up to take Darcy away.

Kim knew that if she showed her true feelings, Darcy would be afraid and she never wanted that child to be afraid again. The little girl had been through so much in her short life, she couldn't put her through more sadness and fear. Of course there were tears cried and the Boydens gave many hugs but as Darcy let the screen door shut behind her, Kim Boyden called out to her, "Darcy sweetie! We're always here if you ever need us. We love you so much." Then she blew her a kiss.

Darcy nodded and waved goodbye as the lady from social services ushered her into the car. As the door closed she noticed that Kim had come out to talk with the large older lady from social services. Darcy could only hear bits of their conversation. The lady was telling Kim, "You knew she may not stay forever. It can't always work out like it did with the last one. Don't push your luck. Some things are better left in the past." The lady smiled and patted Kim on the shoulder as she turned to get into the car. Kim held her hand up to wave as they pulled away from the house.

It turned out that the great job Marsha had was being a waitress at a gentlemen's club on the seedy side of town. Family and Children Protective Services obviously didn't do their homework on this big move of Marsha's. Lancelot's Gentlemen's Club was a dark hole in the wall on a grungy back street. The alley to access the place was so covered in graffiti you could hardly see the entrance. Needless to say, that particular job brought back Marsha's good old Demon Alcohol. It wasn't long before Darcy started to smell the faint odor of liquor on her mom when she would come home in the wee hours of the morning.

9

Darcy questioned her but the excuse was always the same, "I serve alcohol for ten hours a night, of course I'm going to smell like it. I'm NOT drinking if that's what you think." Soon she fell back into her old ways and Darcy spent the next eight years moving around from one dirty, dingy dump to another.

The recently loved and nurtured child from Oklahoma turned into a creature of necessity. She no longer craved her mother's love or even her attention. Darcy learned to fend for herself. She became quite adept at making her own way through the streets of New York and staying out of her mother's way. This situation worked well for Marsha because as time went by, she hardly ever came home at all. She often spent her nights with any man who would buy her a drink which ended at either 'his place,' a dingy motel room, his car or even a back alley. Marsha called it "Doing what I have to do." Darcy called it pathetic.

At sixteen, Darcy got a job at a small diner in Lockport, New York. She waited tables at night while finishing high school and getting her diploma. Once school was finished she landed a full time position at a printing company in the city and moved into her own apartment. It was small with only a large area that included a bed, kitchenette and a small bathroom off to the side. The great thing was, it was cheap.

It was something she could afford on her own with no help from anyone else. Darcy was quite pleased with herself. At least the apartment was much nicer than anything she had ever lived in with her mother. It was an accomplishment to be proud of. The terrible childhood her mother had inflicted on her gave Darcy a better sense of responsibility than most girls her age. Aside from work, she hardly ever went out. She almost never saw her mother and that was the way she liked it. The occasional dinner with a friend was okay but no night life. She knew what that life did to you by watching her mother. Darcy knew she was too smart for that. She would protect herself from that life again at all costs.

Chapter 5

Things started to get into a routine with Darcy. It was a comfortable life that made her feel secure. Her job was great and she had made lots of new friends at work. She even joined a book club with a few of the girls at the office.

Darcy had been settled in comfortably for about two months when she got a call. The call came late one night as she was preparing for bed. It almost felt as if the sound of the ring was different than normal. She felt frozen for the first few seconds. It was as if she knew something was on the other end that she didn't want to face.

No one ever called this late.

She made her way to the phone and answered. It was a man who identified himself as a police officer. She never even heard his name. If she did, she couldn't recall it for the life of her. The man informed her that Marsha, her mother, had been found dead in her bed; possible overdose. According to the officer, the body had been transported to the morgue less than one hour earlier. He assured her that she was welcome to come across town to view the body and make arrangements but there was no need for a formal identification since Marsha was found in her own home with a picture ID on the nightstand.

Darcy thanked the man and hung up. She wasn't sure how Marsha's death made her feel. The numbness was creeping slowly down her body. Her mother had never been very good to her, but on the other hand, she was Darcy's biological mother. The next morning she called a local mortuary with the information they needed to pick up the body for cremation. *No thank you Sir, there will be no service arrangements. The check will be delivered today. Have a great day.*

Soon after her mother's death, she began writing her first manuscript. It was therapeutic for her. She could enter another world when she wrote and leave all the worries of the present behind. A well-known publishing company accepted it almost immediately and within the year she was on her way to becoming a full-fledged author. It was the life she never believed she would have.

Chapter 6

Darcy Scott had long brown hair that almost reached her waist, sparkling green eyes, and an olive complexion that accented her five foot, five inch frame. At twenty-six, she had written three books and was in the process of writing her fourth. She had a flat of her own and an uneventful but comfortable relationship with a man named Michael Marshall. Life had surely turned out to be much better for her than even she would've imagined. She was a long way from dirty back alley apartments and eating out of restaurant dumpsters.

Now, sitting at her desk in her office, she had been thinking of all these things until she heard a loud knock that brought her back to the present.

Bang! Bang! Bang!

She barely had an opportunity to turn the handle completely before Michael strode through the doorway with his usual swagger of confidence. That particular trait was one of the things Darcy usually found adorable about him but today it only irritated her. He interrupted a very happy daydream. Just like a man to ruin a good feeling, she thought.

"How's my beautiful girl today? I have great news. Guess who just got promoted to Foreign Accounts Manager?"

Darcy walked to her desk, picked up her pen, sat down in her chair and leaned back.

"I'm guessing you," she mumbled.

Michael raised an eyebrow at her and crossed his arms. "Gee, don't be too excited. I thought you would be happy for me. What's wrong with you these days? You're zoning out more often and you're always grumpy."

Darcy scowled and flipped back a piece of long brown hair that had escaped from the clip high atop her head.

"Nothing is WRONG with me. I just have a lot on my mind with this book. My deadline is coming up soon and I can't seem to concentrate. People keep interrupting me."

The insinuation that he was the person who kept interrupting her must have flown right over Michael's head because he didn't respond.

Darcy paused and suddenly blurted out, "I've been toying with the idea of taking a little vacation out west. What ya think, maybe to Oklahoma?"

Michael seemed speechless for a moment then slowly responded, "Oklahoma? You don't have time to be happy for me and my promotion but you have time to go to Oklahoma? Explain this to me Darce. What in the world is in Oklahoma? Most people vacation in the islands or overseas or even Disneyland, but Oklahoma? What's this all about?"

Darcy realized that the time had come to be open with Michael about what was going on in her head. She couldn't hold it all in anymore and expect to just skim by on a private existence. She asked him to sit down opposite of her in the plush chair she kept available for the small amount of visitors who graced her office. Michael's tall six foot one frame crossed the room, took his seat, and continued to peer at her through lowered lids. When he gazed at her this way it always made her nervous. His dark eyes seemed almost black when he was worried or concerned. Michael cocked his head to the side and folded his arms. A lock of his blonde hair bobbed as he rocked slightly waiting to hear what she had to say.

Slowly she began the story that summed up 'who is Darcy Scott.' It took almost an hour for her to take him through the painful days of her childhood, the happiness she found on that Oklahoma ranch twenty years earlier and all that came after. He never spoke a word, only stared wide eyed. Michael never asked if Darcy was originally from New York, he just assumed. She never spoke of her parents except to say that her mother had passed away while Darcy was still a teenager. He found it odd that she had never mentioned any extended family but being a writer he just thought she was a private person which is often the case with artistic people. Michael realized that he knew what her favorite ice cream was, how she liked to watch college football in her pajamas, and how her skin smelled after she finished showering but he never knew she had been in a foster home or had suffered such horrible things as a small child. Michael was amazed at the woman he saw sitting before him. His mind was rolling with thought, admiration for how she came out of it so great, how it must have affected her even to this day, and how it was necessary for her to take this trip to heal old wounds. He could live with this. If it was what she needed to get closure, he was fine with it.

Darcy was watching Michael watch her. Finally she couldn't take it anymore, "Well, what do you think? Aren't you going to say anything? I just told you my life story and you just stare at me. You think I'm a freak now don't you?"

Michael looked up at his girlfriend and rubbed his hand over his face in an exhausted fashion. "No Darce. I don't think you are a freak. I think you should have shared this information with me before now. I think if you need to go back to that ranch to find some type of closure or whatever it is that you're looking for, go ahead. I applaud you for facing your past."

Darcy was somewhat surprised. She always thought if anyone knew about her past they would think less of her. She should have known better than that because Michael had always been an understanding man. There wasn't a lot of passion in the last twelve months of seeing one another but he was what some call 'a good catch'. There were times when she wondered what was going on inside his head because he never really shared his innermost thoughts but he seemed to be as well rounded as they come.

Chapter 7

Michael Marshall came from a middle class family who loved Darcy very much. Michael was handsome and hard working. He and his whole family were completely 'apple pie.' Michael was like the old purse you just keep going back to. You go out, buy a new purse, get it home, see that all your things won't fit, it doesn't feel good on your shoulder, the color clashes with most of your outfits, and you throw it in the closet and go back to the one you had. That's Michael, good old convenient, comfy purse. Darcy knew in her heart that it was probably wrong to think of him in that way but it was the truth. Two people together and happy, what more could you ask for?

Michael had been mulling over the idea of asking Darcy to marry him but something always felt wrong so he had been waiting for the right time. Now he was thinking that maybe this had happened for a reason. Darcy could go out west, handle her old issues, come home refreshed, and he could ask her to marry him. They could have a fresh start. The more Michael thought of her trip, the more he was sure it was for the best. This could also give him the time that he needed to tie up some personal issues before he was officially off the market as a bachelor.

Darcy got out of her chair and threw her arms around Michael. "Thank you for understanding. I knew you would! Now I'll give you the congratulations that I owed you before and tell you to go go go and get back to what you were doing so that I can pack. I have a trip to plan."

Michael could see that Darcy was suddenly in a playful mood and eager to get this going so he kissed her sweetly, told her he would call her later, and saw himself out.

Her head was reeling. She had so many people to call

and things to do. She had to call her agent Melissa Sandow, the travel agency, the neighbor Miss Marcus, and scores of other people who could handle some personal issues for her while she was away. Note to self-exchange all plants for a cactus when you return. She decided on a flight the next night which would arrive at Will Rogers World Airport in Oklahoma the following evening and from there she would have to rent a car to take her the 107 miles to Carter. Wow, she was really doing this. The reality hadn't set in yet.

She was packing the last of her toiletries when she felt the fear rise up inside of her. "What am I doing? I'm going somewhere I haven't been in so long to find people who probably won't even know me." Her mind began to wander.

Darcy was playing with one of the other foster children, Maria. Their dolls were pretending to go to a big ball to meet a prince when suddenly a ball came flying through the air and knocked their doll's dance floor over. "Jonah!" Darcy screams. Maria stands up and begins yelling "Miss Kim! Miss Kim! Jonah threw a ball at us!" Kim comes running into the bedroom where the girls are playing and finds Jonah laughing and pointing. "Jonah Boyden! Stop being so mean to your sister! You know you don't throw balls at anyone in this house." Jonah turns really red and faces his mother. "SHE is NOT my sister."

Thoughts of Jonah Boyden made her remember all the mean pranks he played on her as a kid. He was always a spiteful little boy, nothing like his older brother Davis. She couldn't recall Davis ever saying a mean thing to her. Oh well, everyone grows up and matures. She was sure that Jonah would be a much nicer adult than he was as a child.

All through the flight Darcy was a bundle of nerves and it only got worse when her plane landed. There were moments when she considered staying glued to her seat and letting the plane fly her back to the place where she lost her common sense. It seems that the airline frowns on people being forcibly removed from their aircrafts so she got off the plane and made her way over to the rental car counter. After handing over her credit card and all her information she traveled through the parking lot out back looking for her 2003 Ford Focus. Not the sexiest car alive but it would do for what she needed. Great gas mileage was always a plus. She grabbed her map and took off.

Chapter 8

It was an interesting drive. Twenty years changes things a lot and she passed places that never existed when she was last there and she passed others that she even remembered. About an hour and a half later she was entering the town of Carter. Darcy passed through the familiar streets until she reached the old road leading out to the Boyden place.

'I cannot believe I'm doing this. Maybe I'm having an early midlife crisis or I've simply gone insane, full blown." Thoughts roared through her mind at warp speed. No feeling so far had prepared her for what she was feeling when she rolled up to the front gate. Memories flooded her from all sides. It felt as if all the air had been sucked out of her lungs and replaced with hot coal dust. Her eyes greedily consumed the scene before her.

A small blonde haired girl and a skinny brown haired boy with freckles played on the swing hanging from the giant tree to Darcy's left. A third child was carefully watering a pretty little bed of flowers beside the front porch. It appeared that Albert and Kim were still touching the lives of abandoned and abused children. It made a tear come to Darcy's eye and a smile played on her lips.

Suddenly, out of the corner of her eye she saw it. There after all these years was the rope bridge. Just the sight of it made Darcy's bottom lip quiver. Oh how she longed to live here forever, to stay with these wonderful people and never have to go back to that cold hard life her mother had doomed her to.

'I should go, just leave. Accept that I cannot go back and go home where I belong. Yes, that's what I will do and when I get home I will try to forget that I ever did this.' Her thoughts were beginning to sound saner by the minute.

All of a sudden she realized that someone was standing at the driver's window of her car. Dear Lord! It startled her enough for her to visibly jump up in her seat. She rolled the window down and looked straight at the man standing there eyeing her suspiciously. Apparently the Stranger Danger class she had in elementary school didn't stick or she wouldn't have considered rolling down her window at this moment. If Darcy had to guess he was probably around 6 foot, dark hair much like her own and one of the most strikingly handsome men she had ever seen. Of course Ted Bundy was a handsome guy too so the serial killer idea was still on the table. Jeez! What was she thinking? OK. Calm down Darcy and stop behaving like an idiot. Like a haze that was being lifted she began to realize that beyond this man's visible good looks and the idea that he may be a raving lunatic, there was something familiar about him.

When Darcy didn't seize the chance to speak, he did. "Is there something I can do for you?" His right eyebrow lifted in an inquiring way. Was this lady lost? Maybe. All he could tell at this moment was that she was at the very least confused. Darcy opened her mouth to speak but she was so nervous nothing seemed to come out. The dark haired man crossed his arms like a petulant child. He didn't have all day to wait for her answer. Finally realizing that she was already too late to turn and run, she said, "I uh, well, see, I uh, I'm here to see Albert and Kim. Are you a friend of theirs?"

The man, still looking at her uneasily, replied, "No, I'm their oldest son Davis. Who might you be?" Surely this situation was not as awkward as it seemed. OK, it really was. Not only had she made an imbecilic decision to travel all this way to a place where she didn't belong, but now, right when she was on the cusp of rectifying that decision, she gets caught by an actual member of the Boyden family. She must really look like a moron to this person. If not, she truly felt like a moron herself. Oh well, what's done is done. No going back on the plan now. Time to move forward.

Chapter 9

Darcy was shocked at the revelation that this man in front of her was the young boy she once knew. Now she saw the connection. Twenty years had changed the once scrawny little boy into a very handsome man. There were definitely many broken hearts throughout high school for Davis Boyden.

Darcy finally found her voice and clearly answered, "My name is Darcy Scott. I stayed with you and your family 20 years ago through the foster family system. I'm sure you don't remember me and this sounds unusual but well, see..." Her fingers drummed nervously on the steering wheel as she tried not to sputter out a small version of her story.

A smile broke out on Davis' face and suddenly recognition lit up his eyes. He interrupted her quickly, "Oh my goodness! Little Darcy Scott. I didn't recognize you at first. Wow! You certainly have grown up. Wait right here for just a minute. Let me open the gate and you can pull up to the house. I know Mom will be so happy that you've come. She's going to freak out."

This was strange. This man was acting as if she left last year, not twenty years ago. The idea of who was the crazy one was beginning to change for her. It may not be too late to throw the car into reverse and take off. Shake it off Darcy. Focus.

This was all becoming too much for Darcy to process. It was possible that he could actually remember her. It could also be possible that Davis was just being nice and really thinks I'm a deranged intruder, she thought with a nervous laugh. It was hard to think she had any impact on people since all her life she had never meant much to anyone or at least that was how it felt.

He ran ahead of the car and opened the gate. Darcy

pulled through and drove the rest of the way up to the main house.

All the children outside stopped to look her way; probably wondering if she were a social worker coming to move them to another home without notice. That was an unfortunate fear of children who are in the system. Many times she could recall one of her foster brothers or sisters crying because Kim had come in to explain that the 'Nice Lady' would be coming to take them somewhere different. It was never a happy time for any of them. Living the life of a tiny vagabond was hard.

Darcy was lucky that she got to stay the entire time with the Boydens. That was until she was sent back to her mother which turned out to be worse than just being shipped to a different foster home.

Darcy smiled and waved to each one but they turned away and continued to play their games. Strangers were treated with caution in their world. In the meantime Davis had already run into the house yelling for his mother. His voice could be heard booming across the yard.

When Darcy reached the top step of the porch she looked up and there in front of her was Kim Boyden. She was of course older but there was no mistaking who this lady was.

Kim was heavier with gray streaking her short dark hair. She wore a half apron around her considerable waist to catch any loose cooking ingredients since it appeared that she had been cooking when she was called away from her kitchen. "Darcy girl, you came home!" Kim exclaimed. "Let me look at you darling." The older lady had tears in her eyes and one hand partially covering her mouth in awe.

Darcy had no idea that this woman ever thought of her or even remembered her. Darcy hesitated at first and then she bounded up that last step and into Kim's arms. The woman squeezed her so tight she could hardly breathe. That was fine though because if she died right on the spot it would have been worth it to be hugged in such a wonderful way.

"Oh it's so good to see you. I wasn't sure you would even know who I was. I just had to come see this place again." Darcy was struggling for her words because she had the overwhelming urge to cry her heart out.

Kim held her at arm's length, staring straight into her eyes and said, "Honey, we had you for over two years. You were like one of our own. You stayed with us longer than any of the other children ever did or ever have since then. We even discussed adopting you if the option ever became available. You know, if your mom ever gave up her rights completely. It broke my heart when they came here and took you away. Oh I hoped for your sake that your mom really had changed and would give you a good life but that little piece of me wanted you to stay right here with us forever. We tried to write to you but the children's services told us you had moved away with no forwarding address. It wasn't policy for them to give contact information out anyway but I tried. We always prayed you would come back here one day so we could see what a beautiful young lady you turned out to be." Kim grabbed her hand to lead her through the house.

Darcy followed Kim and Davis into the home that she knew all too well. This wasn't just a house. This was a home. There was no other place on the earth that she had ever felt this feeling at before.

Chapter 10

Once inside they sat on the couch and simply caught up on the past twenty years. Darcy couldn't help but to recall the times that all the kids had crowded on that same yellow and brown plaid couch. She looked to her left at the narrow stair case with the worn down brown shag carpeting, worn down from the many little feet running over it throughout the years. It even smelled the same. The smell was a mixture of baking bread and freshly washed laundry. The aroma was almost intoxicating. It made you want to throw off your shoes and sit cross legged on the rug.

It was to Darcy's sadness to find out that Albert had passed away the previous fall. He had succumbed to pneumonia brought on by an autoimmune disease. It was just Kim, Davis, and the foster children.

She could tell that Kim was still very lonely without her husband. The two of them were first loves who married right out of high school. They never spent a night apart until Albert was hospitalized. Even during those days Kim only came home at night to be here for the other children while her sons took turns staying overnight with their father.

Davis had married but it didn't work out and he was currently divorced. Much like his mother and father, Davis married his high school sweetheart. They were the towns 'it' couple. While Davis went to law school, his young wife worked up quite a client list doing hair at a local salon. The marriage fell apart quickly when real life began. After divorcing, Davis moved home to help with his ailing father and decided to stay on after he passed and help his mom. Davis had now become an accomplished attorney, to Darcy's surprise. She could tell how proud of him his mother was.

Kim leaned in and whispered, "Davis makes time at least once every day to help me out with something big. He's such a good boy. His father was so proud." Darcy didn't blame her for bragging about her son in such a way. He seemed to have become a great man.

Davis chimed in praises for his younger brother Jonah who had moved out of town to be an investment banker.

"Don't forget, Mom, to tell her what a success Jonah is. That boy has come a long way." Kim smiled and patted her son's knee.

"Of course I wouldn't forget your brother." She looked at Darcy sheepishly "I'm a proud mom of both my boys." Darcy nodded, "I'm sure you are."

It must be amazing to have a mom who is so proud of what you do, she thought. Marsha never acknowledged anything Darcy did unless it was wrong and she could scream at her for it. The large part of Darcy's drive for success was to make herself feel some worth that her mother never showed her. Sad but true.

Jonah Boyden, the younger son, was married with one child, a boy named after himself and his father, Albert Jonah Boyden, which everyone called AJ.

Davis bragged on his nephew as if he were the world's smartest and cutest child ever. The smile was big but the words were laced with a note of sadness and Darcy wondered if he had ever wished for children with his ex-wife. Maybe she was reading too much into it. Maybe he just missed his nephew being so far away. That's what being a close-knit family meant; loved from near or far. The chit chat went on for more than two hours. For the first time in twenty years Darcy felt like she was part of a real family. The warm feeling had spread throughout her chest and into her hands. This was nice, really nice. Too bad it had to end so soon.

"Kim, I just want to thank you for welcoming me and letting me visit with you all again. I don't want to impose any longer. I really have to get to my hotel and get settled."

Kim looked as if she were going to cry at any moment and said, "I was hoping you would stay with us while you were in town for the week. There's so much more to talk about. Surely, you will come back won't you? I've waited all these years for you to return and it just seems like there isn't enough hours in the day."

Darcy became silent. Staying here would mean more to her than they knew but she needed to keep her distance so that leaving would not be so hard when the week was over.

At that time Davis spoke up, "Yes, Darcy you really should come spend some real time with us this week. We would love to have you." Davis' eyes looked so inviting that Darcy just couldn't say no. She left the ranch with a promise made that she would return the next day.

Davis Boyden watched Darcy drive through the gate and out of sight. He walked down the drive to shut the gate with his mind still in disbelief. What made her want to come back here after all these years? She made no comments about kids or a husband. Could it be that she was still single? Davis being thirty-two years old was six years her senior which was a big difference when they were kids. She was eight when he was fourteen.

He thought she was a cute kid and very polite but he never really paid her much attention. Fourteen year old boys have too much going on to care much about eight year old fostered siblings. He just couldn't seem to take his attention away from her today. Davis shook his head to rid himself of all the thoughts jumping into his brain.

He hadn't actually felt an attraction to any woman since his divorce. This was a new feeling for him. Oh dear Lord! Why did it have to be someone that was like family? He needed to get himself into line. She's family, she's family, he just kept telling himself.

Chapter 11

Katie had ruined it for Davis Boyden. Katie Latham had been his high school sweetie. She was an excitable, beautiful cheerleader and everyone loved her, especially Davis. His whole world seemed to revolve around her. He never even had a chance to date anyone else in school like most boys his age did. Nope, Katie was all he ever wanted.

They married right out of high school and she stuck with him all through law school. Katie took a course at the local tech school for cosmetology. Once she got her certificate she started doing hair in town at Golda's salon. The only argument they ever had was when Davis would mention how it might be nice to go ahead and start a family. That subject seemed to be the trigger every time. Katie would become sullen and declare, "Can't we have something for ourselves before we bring a baby into this?" It would end with Davis eating dinner alone while Katie went out with friends.

He was never quite sure what she meant by that comment, "have something for ourselves," because he thought that a baby *would* be something for themselves. Obviously Katie didn't see it that way. He just continued to hope that when he started his own practice she would be more receptive to the idea.

The day that Davis signed the lease on the new building that would house his law practice, he ran excitedly down the two blocks to Golda's Hair and Tan where Katie worked as a stylist. He was so happy to be able to tell his wife that they could begin their new lives. This was going to be the turning point. He would be practicing law like he always dreamed and the money would be coming in. He would even be able to buy Katie her own salon after they got their first child out of diapers.

The ideas for their future were unlimited. He couldn't wait to share it all with his beautiful wife.

When he walked into the shop he scanned the chairs for Katie and didn't see her. Her chair was second from the door but it didn't look like she was working at it today. One of the other girls wordlessly motioned to the back office behind the counter.

Davis nodded and headed for the rear of the shop. He grabbed the door handle to open the door and suddenly he realized Katie was inside on the phone. He could hear her quietly talking, "Yes, baby I know you're tired of waiting but if I kick Davis out right now we will have to pay for the house. It's close to being paid off. If we let him pay it off I can kick him out, divorce him, and then we can be together like we should be. Trust me. We're going to be so happy and we can start a family. You know how bad I want to have your babies." Her giggle rippled through the air lightly.

Davis felt a hot wave shoot from his stomach up into his face. His mind couldn't process what he just heard. She's cheating on me. She wants to have someone else's baby. How long has this been going on? All these thoughts hit him at once. He couldn't breathe. He heard Katie chuckling as he turned the knob on the door. When it opened she had her feet propped on the desk with the phone to her ear. The smile on her face evaporated. It seemed that every ounce of love he had for this woman had just turned into hate. His rational mind told him that this was no misunderstanding and she could have no explanation for what he just heard, at least no acceptable explanation. His face must have looked like a plaster mask of fury because that's exactly how he felt, furious.

"I got to call you back," she told her unknown lover on the phone. "Davis, what are you doing here? I'm working!" Katie snarled. Like always, she thought she could control the moment just like she controlled every other aspect of her husband. It appeared that she was used to being the one who 'ran the show.'

Davis began to speak in a low strained voice, "Really? Is that what you call it? So you have decided to make a career out of being a whore?"

Alarm lit up her face. "What the hell are you talking about? How dare you!" she spat as she jumped up from her chair.

"Don't play games with me Katie. I heard every word of your nasty little phone conversation to your boyfriend. I don't know who he is and I really don't care. I see now that all the time I've put into you has been a waste. I want you to come to the house, get all your stuff, and get the hell out. I'll be drafting our divorce papers first thing in the morning."

Katie was still standing there with a dumbfounded look on her face when Davis slammed the door on his way out. That was the end of his marriage and since then he hadn't found the ability to even look at other women.

Last he heard Katie was shacked up with a different man every month, still working as a hair stylist. It seemed that her master plan to take him for all he was worth blew up in her face. He just believed that it was good proof that you never really know someone. The woman he thought he would love forever had torn his heart out of his chest with no regard.

Chapter 12

When Darcy got to her hotel that night she was exhausted. All the excitement of the day had taken its toll on her. Her legs ached and her back was stiff. She put away her things in the bathroom, brushed out her hair, and unpacked a few pairs of jeans before taking a hot shower.

It seemed as if the shower washed away all the anxiety she had been carrying on the plane ride. Hot steamy water really was the miracle cure. She toweled off and donned a fluffy blue robe. Feeling weightless and relaxed she decided to give Michael a call and fill him in on the visit. She was sure he would be eager to hear from her.

Darcy dialed the number and after three rings, he answered, "Hey Darce! How did it go?" She started to tell Michael all about it and the words just kept coming. He didn't even get an opportunity to speak for the first few minutes. Her excitement was obvious. He listened closely as she related every detail; obviously she was pleased with her trip so far.

Michael was so happy that it went well. He really was. He knew how much it meant to her. He was even surer now that his idea to ask Darcy to marry him was solid. They could finally be totally happy now that he knew what was bothering her and it had been dealt with. He constantly felt as if there were a large wall between him and her. A wall he always climbed to the top of and just when he thought he might make it over, he fell back to the ground. Now, they were unencumbered. Although he had not spoken to her of marriage he was sure she felt the same way. This was going to be the catalyst to their new life just as soon as she came home.

When Michael found a space in which to speak, he jumped in and said, "So...now that all that is over, you going to head on home or take in a day's worth of shopping while you're there?"

She spoke in a puzzled tone, "No, I told you I wanted to spend a week. Remember? Kim invited me to come back and spend some time this week and I accepted. I will be home next week. Is that a problem?" She couldn't explain why she suddenly felt so defensive. His tone of voice had rubbed a raw nerve that she didn't even know was there.

Michael thought surely that since everything went well she would be all too eager to come running home to him but he wouldn't be too hurt, it was only one week. He didn't want anything to spoil her mood because he wanted it all to be perfect when she returned home. "No, no problem Darce. You enjoy yourself. I'm going to turn in for the night and I'll talk with you tomorrow. I love you babe."

"Back at ya," she said. That was her usual goodbye when Michael told her he loved her. She wasn't a very lovey dovey type of girl so 'back at ya' was as good as it got from her.

She cradled the phone and suddenly realized that she had made no mention of Davis being there. She told Michael every single detail about her visit except she totally left Davis out of the equation. Strange, she felt kind of guilty and couldn't understand why. He had been like an older brother at one time. It was silly to think that she might be attracted to him. Surely Michael wouldn't feel threatened. The question her subconscious was asking was 'would Michael think you are attracted to Davis out of male competition or because you actually are?' She flushed the thought from her mind as she cuddled up on the chaise near the window. Before long Darcy was dreaming sweet dreams of a rope bridge and a young dark haired boy.

Chapter 13

The morning dawned bright and early the next day. Darcy didn't realize she had fallen asleep and slept the entire night on the chaise. She slept so soundly she wasn't even sore. Her energy level was off the charts this morning. In no time, she was up, dressed in a pair of snug jeans with a ripped knee, and a plain white tee shirt. Darcy slipped her white tennis shoes on and jogged across the street to the closest diner. She grabbed a bite of breakfast and headed out to the ranch.

When she arrived Kim offered her breakfast but she declined, explaining that she had already eaten. Kim started to talk, "Darcy dear I am so sorry but I won't be able to visit with you today. Little Donna here has a terrible cold and I have to take her to the doctor. Davis is around here somewhere though and I'm sure he would be more than glad to entertain you. I really do feel bad about this. I was so looking forward to you and I doing more catching up." The small feverish child in Kim's lap whimpered, making Darcy feel sympathy for her.

"No, please don't feel bad about it. I understand completely. We've got the rest of the week. You just take care of this pretty little imp for now." Little Donna smiled up at her when she heard her refer to her as an imp. The little girl wasn't sure what an imp was but it sounded sweet.

Immediately the thought of spending the day alone with Davis Boyden was playing with Darcy's senses but she knew if she declined it would hurt Kim's feelings and make her look like a real jerk. A light nausea was starting to grow inside her tummy.

As if he could hear her heart beating, Davis walked into the kitchen with an amused look. "Good morning Darcy. I guess Mom told you about having to take Donna to the doctor huh? I'm going to be around if you want to hang with me." See, simple. Just a brother figure offering to show his defacto sister around. Who are you kidding? If it were really like that you wouldn't feel so weird. Darcy shook her head to make her inner voice shut up. Now was not the time to hear that stuff. She would wrestle herself internally later on. She grinned politely at Davis.

"Don't you have to go in to work", Darcy asked.

"Actually, you're in luck. You showed up right as I took a week off to handle some personal issues," he said. His eyes twinkled behind the raised coffee cup. Was she imagining it or was he having fun at her expense?

"Oh, OK, well, I would love to hang with you as you call it if you're sure I won't be in your way," Darcy replied.

Davis sat his coffee cup on the counter with a thud. "It's a date then." Oh no, the urge to vomit just came back, thought Darcy.

Kim packed up the feverish little girl and headed out for the doctor's office.

"I would love the company and the help if you don't mind getting your hands dirty with a little yard work," Davis said. Now he was speaking her language. She loved being outside working the ground. It was something she had missed greatly when she was taken to the city. There were times when she and her mother would have an apartment with a 10X10 patch of grass out back. She could remember trying to get flowers to grow so that their grass would be pretty. She craved a little beauty in the ugly world she lived in.

Darcy jumped right in helping Davis plant flowers, prune trees, and other yard work. She hadn't worked out in the fresh air in so long. To feel the earth between her fingers was exhilarating. The day sped by so fast that before they realized it, they had been working and talking all day. Davis told her all about his work and she shared

35

her love for writing. They covered everything about music, politics, and many other world views. They seemed to cover everything except their personal lives. It was by far the best day Darcy had participated in for many years. Around 5:30, Kim yelled out the back door, "Got a meal cooked if you two are hungry!"

Darcy's face was flushed with the sun she had gotten that day, her hair windblown, and Davis was absolutely taken with her. She noticed him looking intensely at her. Suddenly the familiarity was replaced by tension. "So, are we going to go eat? If I remember right, your mom is the best cook in this area. Is something wrong?" She was positive she had never seen anyone look at her the way he was right now, not even Michael.

Davis spoke before he thought and uttered, "Nothing is wrong. I just don't think I ever saw anyone as beautiful as you look right now." Crap! Did he really just say that out loud or was he hallucinating? Nope, from the look on her face he could tell that he did indeed say it for her to hear. How do you cover that one up as a slip of the lip? He was frozen for fear of what she might say to him.

Darcy was speechless for a minute as well. She was sure he could hear her pulse beating in her ears as loudly as she herself could at that moment. She tried laughing it off and replied, "I guess I am a long way from the skinny little girl with scabs on my knees and hair tha…."

Davis kissed Darcy right square on the lips. Her hands came up around the back of his neck while his hands came to rest on her hips. Momentary lapse of common sense. What in the hell were both of them thinking?

Finally, Davis broke away first and said, "Oh God, I am so sorry. I had no right to do that. I couldn't help myself. Please don't be mad. I don't know what came over me." He raked his hand through his dark hair and she could see the glisten of sweat on his forehead.

Darcy looked down at the ground shyly and responded, "It's OK. No harm no foul. Maybe we should go in before

Kim comes looking for us. She will think we don't want dinner. I for one am famished." Darcy turned and sprinted off quickly ahead of Davis. She was so ashamed of her reaction to his kiss. She had acted too fast. She never reacted like that to Michael. What was going on with her? Michael's face just kept flashing in her mind. Michael, her loving and devoted boyfriend. Guilt was creeping up on her and her thoughts were fuzzy as she entered through the back door. No words were spoken as she washed her hands to eat.

Chapter 14

Dinner was served and the conversation was animated. It really lightened Darcy's mood to have everyone around. All six of the children talked of their day and told funny stories, even the little girl named Donna who had been feeling sick that morning. It's funny how kids bounce back. They can be deathly ill one moment and playing tea party the next. Was this what it was like to have kids and a family? She wasn't sure it got any better than this.

Darcy talked to everyone about how she became a writer and how it was much more work than she ever imagined it would be but she loved it none the less. Davis never looked directly at her through the entire meal. He must think she was awful for being so quick to jump over a simple little kiss. It was okay because she kept her eyes averted from him also.

When dinner was finished and it was time to part, everyone said their goodbyes and goodnights except Davis. He had cleared his place at the dinner table and disappeared over thirty minutes earlier. If anyone noticed the odd behavior, no one mentioned it. Thank goodness. The day's events would be really hard to explain.

Darcy thanked Kim for the food, the great company and assured her she would see them all the next day. She told each child goodnight and she gathered her purse. Strange but she felt a bit of sadness that she couldn't tell Davis goodbye. The chilly breeze blew as she walked to her car. It made her shiver slightly. Just before she opened her car door she looked across the yard and noticed the old rope bridge shining in the evening sun. It was great to see that some things hadn't changed. It seemed that the old bridge was the only thing that had not because she certainly had.

The whole drive back to the hotel she couldn't think about anything but that kiss. If she were a drinking woman she believed she would stop for a drink to clear her head; but a drinker she was not. Sleep may not be easy to come by tonight, she thought. She didn't even have a clue that Davis was somewhere doing the same kind of thinking. The difference was that he actually did have a stiff drink in hand. It would be a long night for each of them.

Chapter 15

Jonah Boyden swirled the ice in his glass around and around slowly. He had been sitting in his chair staring out the window for an hour. The street outside his house was busier today than normal. Watching people go by helped him think clearly. He knew he really needed to take a trip out to his mother's house soon to check on her but he wasn't looking forward to it. He loved his mom but he didn't like a lot of things about his childhood home. It really bothered him how she continued to take in all those homeless brats even after his dad died. He tried to tell her, "Mom, those kids are NOT your responsibility. Send them packing and take care of yourself for a change," but she wouldn't listen. She was too old for that crap at her age. It also got his blood pressure up to know that his older brother Davis had moved home. His brother had his own place a few miles from his mom but he was out at the ranch so often he might as well have moved home. Davis was always the golden child. It made Jonah look bad for his brother to be so annoyingly perfect. He was a big time lawyer who helped his mother daily, according to her constant glowing praise on the telephone. Jonah could almost see the clouds part and shine light on Davis' halo every time he was around. He guessed it wouldn't hurt to take his wife and son down for a visit. If he didn't at least make an appearance often, his brother could tell everyone how he was the only one who helped their mom. What a crock! He reached over on the side table and grabbed his cell phone. Davis wasn't the only one who could be a good son. He flipped it over in his palm a couple of times before he dialed his wife, Michelle's, number.

"Hi babe. When you get home you need to pack all three of us a bag. We're going to mom's for the weekend. Yeah, you, I, and A.J. and we'll stay a couple of days.

OK, see ya soon." Jonah flipped his phone closed and thought a moment.

He decided he needed to call and let Mom know they were coming. They wouldn't stay at the house because he couldn't handle all those kids driving him insane nor did he like A.J. playing with the little ingrates. He scrolled down on his phone listing until he got to 'Mom' and hit call. Why didn't she let him get her a cell phone? He hated calling the home phone because she was so rarely the one who answered. If he wanted to talk to his brother he would call him directly.

The phone rang a few times and just as Jonah thought he would, Davis answered, "Hello, Boyden residence."

"What's up brother? I'm looking for Mom. She around?" Jonah asked.

"Hey Bro! No, Mom's out shopping. Something up?"

"Well actually, I have just been so worried about Mom and it bothers me so much that we don't get to see her often. A.J. just misses his Grammy so bad. So the three of us are coming down for the weekend. We're leaving out tonight."

Davis was surprised at how heartfelt his brother sounded considering he was usually the most self-centered, selfish person you could ever meet. It didn't aggravate him though, because he knew that no matter how much praise he and his parents gave Jonah it was never enough. He had been a constant pain in the behind growing up.

"Good. Mom will be so glad to see you guys. I'll let her know that you're coming. Hey, while I got you on the phone, guess who came to see us and is spending some time here this week?"

Jonah's interest was piqued, "Who?"

"Darcy Scott. Remember her? She came back to see us all and man, she has grown up to be a great girl. She'll be really excited to see you again."

Jonah was almost in shock, "You mean that ratty little

girl that Mom and Dad took in when we were kids?" Jonah wasn't sure if he should laugh or be outraged.

Davis sounded offended, "Yes, the cute little girl that lived with us for over two years. You can at least be nice to her. She's a lovely lady and quite the successful author these days. I'll tell Mom you're coming. Drive safe." With that, Davis hung up. Jonah could push buttons Davis never seemed to know he even had until they were pushed.

Jonah was flabbergasted. What in the hell was that girl doing coming around after all these years? She wasn't even related to them. How could Mom let her hang around? For all they knew she could've turned into a serial killer or a drug dealer! Successful author my ass! The more Jonah fumed on the subject, the madder he got. He suddenly realized that his brother had sounded offended like he had a thing for this girl. Now the situation was becoming humorous. Poor old Davis. His wife stepped out on him and now he thinks he's found love with some strange orphan girl. Jonah could see the possibilities for a good time this weekend. Finally he had a way to make his perfect brother's life not so perfect.

Chapter 16

Darcy showed up at the ranch bright and early the next day. She and Kim had decided to go through some boxes up in the attic and reminisce. It was amazing how much junk they had kept from the kids who had stayed with them. Most of the toys of course had been passed on to the other children but little mementos like finger paintings, popsicle stick houses, and other childhood treasures obviously meant a lot to Kim. It seemed that she had kept most of them.

Kim took a break from unloading an old dusty box, looked up at Darcy and smiled, "You know the first time I saw one of your books in the store, my heart just swelled up with pride. I thought about writing the publishing company and asking them to forward a letter to you. Albert told me not to. He said 'Let the girl be Kim, she's got a whole other life. She may not even want to hear from us.' So I didn't write but I bought your first book, then your second, and so on. You are so talented honey. I'm so glad you're here." She reached over the open box and patted Darcy on the knee.

As she flipped through a stack of refrigerator paintings something fell out and fluttered to the attic floor. Darcy bent over to pick it up and realized it was a picture. The picture was obviously old and a little bit faded from being packed away but in it was a small child who resembled Darcy at that age. She looked like she was around three or four years of age. Squatted down beside the child was a dark haired man that Darcy had never seen before. He didn't look like he could be more than twenty years old and something about him was crazy familiar.

"Kim, who is this?" Darcy asked as she passed the picture over to her.

As soon as Kim laid eyes on the photo she went a bit

pale and stuttered, "Oh that old thing isn't even mine. I think we found it in one of the children's left over belongings once they left."

"This isn't me? It really looks a lot like me."

"No no dear. It couldn't be you. You didn't come to us until you were much older than this child."

Darcy knew that fact but she still couldn't understand how this kid looked so much like she did at that age. She was being silly. How could the Boyden's have gotten a picture of her that young anyway? She hardly had any photos of herself as a small child. Family pictures were not a real high priority for her mom.

It wasn't much longer before they wrapped up their treasure hunting and when they finished in the attic they made their way into the kitchen for lunch. Kim was whipping up one of her special recipes of chicken soup and grilled cheese when Davis came through the door. Darcy felt her heart skip a beat.

"Hi you guys. You been busy this morning?" he asked.

"Oh yes. Darcy and I have been going through some things in the attic. We were pooped and needed some lunch. You hungry dear?" Kim replied.

"No Mom I'm not really hungry. I see Jonah isn't here yet. Hello Darcy. How are you today?"

Davis turned to look at Darcy and she shyly answered, "I'm just fine. Is Jonah coming today?"

He wasn't aware that his mother didn't tell her about his brother coming down. "Yes, Jonah, his wife Michelle, and their son A.J. should be here anytime."

Darcy was never really close to the youngest Boyden son. He tried to steer clear of her it seemed and was always a bit snobby. It would be nice to see how he grew up and meet his wife. Just as Darcy was thinking about such things she heard the front door slam and a loud voice call out, "Mom! We're here!"

It was Jonah. He glided into the kitchen heading straight for Kim.

Jonah was about an inch shorter than Davis. He had the same dark hair and lean build but Darcy noticed that his hands looked like he hadn't done a hard day's work ever. He had hands that were obviously manicured regularly. He looked quite confident in his cream colored polo shirt and chinos.

Jonah hugged his mother briefly and turned to size up his older brother. He looked Davis up and down. Obviously he was criticizing the fact that his brother was wearing jeans and an old college tee-shirt.

"Davis," was all Jonah said. Davis nodded his head in acknowledgment turned and picked up the toddler who was hanging onto the leg of the kitchen table.

"Michelle, good to see you," Davis said. Michelle smiled brightly at him. As Davis began to tickle and make funny noises to the baby, Jonah turned to Darcy.

"Well, well, if it isn't Darcy Scott. You look too old to have been brought here by a social worker again so what brings you to our family's doorstep this time?"

Darcy turned slightly pink and answered, "I was always fond of your family and I wanted to come visit. Everyone has been quite welcoming to me after all these years."

Jonah snorted, "Yeah, that's us, real welcoming."

Before Darcy could respond Davis spoke up, "Darcy, I have to go into town, would you like to ride with me?"

He sat the baby back down beside his mother and turned toward the door. Darcy jumped up with her head lowered, "Sure. I'll get my purse." Any excuse to escape such an awkward situation was fine with her, even if it meant alone time with Davis.

As Davis walked by his brother he saw the twinkle in his eye. Jonah was always great at making an uncomfortable moment. Kim didn't even bother to ask why they weren't staying for lunch. She knew it was Jonah's behavior. Her prayer was always the same, that there would come a day when her younger son would find enough inner peace to treat others with something other than contempt. At times she wondered how she went wrong with him.

Chapter 17

Darcy returned with her purse and they swiftly made their exit out the back door. Once they had gotten into the car, Davis spoke.

"I'm really sorry about my brother's mouth. He never has been able to use tact. Ignore him. The family is really happy you're here, especially me."

Davis almost couldn't believe that he just said that to her. She looked up startled. Suddenly he leaned over and kissed her lightly on the lips, lingering for just a moment. It felt as if the oxygen had been removed from the inside of the car. As he pulled back from her he spoke softly, "I won't apologize for that one. Seeing you these last couple of days has struck a spark in my heart I never thought I would feel again. Please tell me that you feel it, that I'm not alone in this madness."

It took a minute for her to be able to speak. Darcy's mind was running too fast with thoughts of her home, Michael, and so much more. "Davis, I have to admit, I feel the same way. I just don't know what to do about it. I'm confused right now." She knew she had caused this by refusing to tell him about Michael. Did she invite it on purpose? Was that why she failed to mention that she was in a committed relationship? Committed was a word that was making her feel like the scum of the earth right now. Dear God, what had she done?

Davis nodded and said, "I can understand. I just want you to know that I think God sent you back to us for me. I know that sounds selfish but just give it a chance.... Stay with me tonight Darcy." He had never been so impetuous in his entire life and it felt good. He always knew that there was something out there for him like this. He had loved Katie but it had been a safe and secure love. It wasn't the kind of love that made you feel like your lungs constrict and your body temperature sky rockets. Those feelings were what he felt when he was with Darcy.

She looked deep into his eyes and found herself uncontrollably nodding her head and saying "Yes."

He said nothing, only smiled. Neither of them wanted to jinx the moment. It was mostly silent on the short trip into town. Darcy's mind roaring with all the horrible words Michael would be calling her right now if he knew what she was planning. Davis was thinking how he must be losing his mind to do this. They picked up some supplies from the hardware store and headed back.

When they returned to the ranch, Darcy explained to Kim that she had some business to take care of and needed to go back to her hotel. Kim was sad but she couldn't blame the girl. It was obvious after the way Jonah treated her that she wouldn't want to be near him. That boy had always had a rude streak no matter how much she and Albert had taught him about manners. He was her baby but this was by far not the first time she had been ashamed and embarrassed by his behavior.

Darcy said her goodbyes with kisses and hugs and headed to her car. As she was backing out she noticed Jonah sitting on the porch watching her. Something in his eyes told her that not only did he not like her but he seemed to be studying her. It sent chills down her spine. This whole episode had surely made her paranoid. This was not the day to let herself be concerned with the opinion of someone who didn't even want her around. She had much more pressing issues to deal with, one of which would be the upcoming event of cheating on her boyfriend. Darcy had never even entertained the idea of cheating on Michael until now and her common decency said that now was not the time to start. She had to tell Davis the truth tonight. It couldn't wait any longer. She turned the car and pulled out of the driveway.

Darcy drug herself from the parking area through the

front entrance of the hotel. She felt so guilty about what was almost about to happen that she could hardly hold her head up. Guilt was a cruel and vicious foe. She hadn't actually done more than share a kiss so far but that coupled with the 'almost' plan of spending the night with another man made her feel as low as she had ever felt in her life.

When she finally made it to her room the telephone was already ringing. She dropped her purse, went over to the nightstand and picked up the phone.

"Hello?"

It was Davis.

"I just wanted to tell you that I will be at your hotel room around seven pm. We didn't actually set a time. You haven't changed your mind have you?"

"No, I haven't changed my mind. I'll see you at seven," she said.

As she hung up the phone on the nightstand she realized that she just had an opportunity to tell Davis over the phone and save her the humiliation of doing it in person. Why didn't she take the chance? The situation was beginning to make her feel very much like a schoolgirl. There was a part of her that was excited and jittery. That would be the part that was NOT feeling like a complete traitor.

She turned to head to the shower when the phone rang again. He forgot something. He changed his mind. There were several reasons he could be calling back but either way, she had to act on it. It was clear to her that if she didn't do this now, she would not do it in person.

"Hello, we need to talk."

The voice that answered was not Davis. It was Michael. "Hi Sweetheart! We certainly do need to talk. I miss my baby. You've hardly called me. So what do we need to talk about? You first."

She was so taken aback that she tried to think fast, "Well, I, uh thought you were the front desk. They called up to ask if I needed any fresh towels and I told them no but I realized I really do need clean towels so.... Oh forget about my silliness. So how are you today? I've missed you Michael. I'm so glad you called."

Michael of course believed her pathetic lie. "I'm great, just missing my baby. I wanted to check in with you. So what are your plans for dinner tonight?" Wow, she's really acting strange tonight. She must be totally homesick. Poor thing, Michael thought.

Darcy felt a stab in her heart when she heard him ask her plans. "I'm thinking about ordering a sandwich and going to sleep early. All this excitement has me wore out."

"Well darling I think that's a great idea. You just get some rest and call me tomorrow. I just really wanted to hear your voice. I'll be so glad when you're finally home. I love you Darce."   "Back at ya," she replied.

Hanging up the phone she almost said 'I'm sorry,' but she choked up. Instead she simply hung up the phone and went to the shower. Time was passing fast and in just a few hours she would be alone with Davis in her hotel room.

Michael had heard a jittery tone in Darcy's voice that he had never heard. He was starting to wonder if this whole thing had been a good idea after all. He thought that at least she would be home soon and when he surprised her she would be ecstatic.

Michael had spent the day with his mother going through every single jewelry store in town looking for just the right ring to present to the woman he wanted to spend the rest of his life with. For days he had been thinking of just the perfect way to propose and now he believed he had it. Originally he had gone over every scenario he could do once she got off that plane but now he had the perfect plan. This plan would take the cake.

Michael would take a plane down to Oklahoma the day

before Darcy was scheduled to come home, show up at the Boyden ranch, and propose right in front of everyone. It would be something that Darcy would never forget the rest of her life.

Chapter 18

Davis was more nervous than he had been the day he married Katie. How could he have been so bold by asking her to stay the night with him? How could she actually accept? He was stunned. Maybe this was a mistake. Maybe he should call her and back out. While he was running around his bedroom in a frenzy, he realized someone was standing just inside the door watching him.

"Jonah, did you need something? You startled me standing there."

His little brother was quiet for a moment then held his index finger up to his mouth and replied, "You look like a man who's going on a date. Anyone I know?"

The aggravation was obvious on Davis' face.

"I don't think it's really any of your business. You only come here to make a show of yourself to Mom so why act like you even like me *little brother?*"

His comment didn't even faze Jonah. "You know, *big brother,* you're going to make a fool of yourself with that woman. I'm not sure if you just have the desire to go slumming or if it's just been so long since you had a woman you'll take anything but I suggest you not embarrass yourself."

Davis' first thought was to punch him in the jaw but he counted to ten in his head before he responded. "Jonah, let me tell you something and I'm only going to tell you one time. Stay out of my business. I am a grown man and it would serve you well to keep your opinions to yourself. You can see yourself out the same way you came in."

With a sympathetic nod, Jonah turned and walked away.

At seven o'clock sharp Darcy heard the knock on her hotel room door. She had her long brown hair swept up in pins, curls falling down around her shoulders, and was wearing a light blue sundress with white sandals. When she opened the door her heart skipped a beat. Davis was there in a dapper dark blue pin striped suit. It was obviously one of his many courtroom attires because he looked quite professional and handsome. His dark hair seemed to be setting off the shine in his eyes.

"Please, come in," she said.

"Thank you. I thought we would go out to dinner. I've made reservations at a lovely Italian restaurant just a few blocks from here," he said as he strolled into the room.

"That's great. I'll just get my wrap and my purse and we can go."

The two headed out of the hotel and decided to walk the distance to the restaurant. It was a beautiful evening. They chatted as they walked and Darcy could only think about what a sweet emotion she was feeling while being with him. It was as if all the tension drained away. In her mind she envisioned him showing up and the two of them falling into bed immediately. It never occurred to her that he just wanted to spend time with her. He wasn't opening the door for any ugly indiscretion. She felt so much better now.

All throughout dinner they talked about childhood, school, his job, her new book, and laughed until they couldn't laugh anymore. As they finished dinner and walked away from the restaurant she was sure this was the best night she had ever had. It was so amazing to be so comfortable with someone.

She had never shared that closeness with any man, not even Michael. There was always a small barrier between Michael and her no matter what she did or didn't do. It was hard to explain but easy to recognize. Strange how you can feel close to the people you least expect.

Once they arrived at the hotel, Davis walked her to her room. Darcy slid the key in the lock of her hotel door and Davis followed her in. Darcy put down her purse and immediately turned to him. "I had the best time tonight. I just want you to know that I started out a little nervous."

Davis looked puzzled, "Why were you nervous?"

Suddenly it dawned on him what she meant. He held his hand out and while shaking his head he spoke, "Oh Lord, you actually thought when I asked you to spend the night with me that I was talking about sex. No Darcy. Do you really think I would disrespect you like that? Don't get me wrong, I am very attracted to you but I want more than that from you. I just want to be with you tonight." He secured his hand around hers and pulled her towards him.

She didn't know what to say. Not once in her life had any man showed her so much respect. Michael had even groped her from their first date forward. She just assumed that all men were the same.

Davis walked over to the television and turned it on. He slid off his jacket and his shoes and lay back on the bed and patted the space beside him. "I won't bite. I just thought we could watch some late night shows," he said.

This man must be a dream because she felt like she was floating on cloud nine. Darcy smiled, pulled out the pins in her hair, slipped off her sandals, and climbed on the bed beside him. She snuggled up close and after only a few minutes she was sound asleep.

Around nine o'clock the next morning Darcy's eyes fluttered open. She and Davis had both fallen asleep in their clothes. The spot beside her on the bed was empty. She got up out of the bed and padded across the floor on her bare feet. She noticed a note on the table by the door. It simply read, "Dear Darcy, Thank you for a wonderful night and for the most pleasant sleep I've had in a long time. Hope to see you later today."

A smile came across her face as she read the words he had written. Darcy went to the closet and picked out a pair of denim shorts, a pink tank with little flowers scrolled across the neck line, and a pair of small white canvas shoes. She was going to shower, get a bite to eat, and make her way to the ranch. The answer was suddenly so clear. She was feeling feelings she had never felt before and she couldn't ignore it. Her relationship with Michael was going nowhere and she knew that. For the first time in her life she decided she was going to have to take a chance if she was ever going to be truly happy. The only thing that hurt her was that she would have to break the news to Michael. It was true there was no spark between the two of them but he had been good to her. She would feel bad to let him down but it had to be done. When she returned home it would be the first order of business to talk to Michael.

Darcy went by the diner and picked up breakfast. It was a glorious day. She couldn't be sure if it felt that way because the sun was shining so beautifully or if it was because she felt a connection to a wonderful human being for the first time in her life.

Chapter 19

When she arrived at the ranch the kids were out in the yard running back and forth across the rope bridge playing what appeared to be a pirate game. The sight made a smile come to Darcy's face. She got out of her rental car and walked into the house. Jonah and his family appeared to be there because she noticed their car parked beside the house. When Darcy entered she saw Michelle sitting in the floor with A.J. helping him construct a house out of Legos.

Michelle looked up at Darcy and smiled but quickly looked back down at her son. Darcy got the impression that Michelle was the quiet type who didn't talk to many people. She appeared to be the polar opposite of her husband. Jonah didn't have a problem talking to anyone. Darcy walked through the hallway towards the kitchen hoping to find Kim or Davis. She walked into the kitchen and the only person standing at the counter was Jonah.

He looked at her with a grin across his face, "Darcy, how lovely of you to visit. I'm surprised you could rise this early after showing my brother such a good time that he didn't even come home until sunrise."

Darcy turned a dark shade of pink.

"I'm looking for Kim. I'll just go out back and see if she's with the children," she said as she headed for the back door. As Darcy reached for the knob Jonah darted across the room to grab her wrist.

"Don't go so soon. I thought we could talk for a minute."

She snatched her hand away as if she had been burned, "Jonah, you and I have nothing to talk about. You have made it clear that you don't like me and don't want me here. Davis is a grown man and if he enjoys spending time with me that's his business, not yours. Now, let me go."

Jonah's faced turned dark red and he raised his finger up to Darcy's face. "Let me share some information with you. What goes on with everyone in this family is my business. You are not welcome here and it won't take my brother long to find out what you're really after. I'm not sure what that would be but I'm sure that low born trash like you must have a hidden agenda. I don't care how many books you've written you're still unwanted here. Don't think that I won't make damn sure that you leave soon!" With that being said, Jonah pivoted and walked away.

Darcy was visibly shaking as she walked out back to find Kim or Davis. Right now she would settle for anyone other than that cruel black hearted Jonah Boyden. What a jerk! It was hard to believe that he and Davis were blood related. His wife even appeared to be afraid of him. How tragic!

Kim was swinging peacefully in the wooden swing out back as Darcy came upon her. Kim noticed a tremble all over Darcy's body. "Oh, sweetie, why are you shaking so badly? What's wrong?"

Darcy tried to smile as she sat down beside Kim on the swing. "Nothing at all. I just got a call from an old friend who had a problem but it's solved now." She didn't think Kim believed her but she wasn't about to tell her what her youngest son just did and said. Darcy could never cause Kim any pain on purpose.

The two women sat in silence for several minutes watching three of the younger children chase a butterfly around a large oak tree. Finally it was Kim who broke the silence. "Most people think that I don't see much going on since Albert died but that's just not true. I see lots of stuff like right now I see that you and my son like one another a whole lot. As a matter of fact, I dare say that I see much more in his eyes than friendship. A mother can see these things in her son. I also believe I see the same in you. Just remember, love hasn't been good to Davis in the past. Walk softly. I love you both and I don't want to see either of you hurt."

Wow, she could see it written all over both of them. Was it that obvious? Darcy couldn't speak for a moment. Quiet little Kim Boyden took in everything around her. She was a well of knowledge.

"Kim, this is a new feeling for me also and I promise that I won't ever do anything to intentionally hurt Davis. I swear," Darcy said as tears came into her eyes.

At that moment a voice came from behind. "I'm going into town to get ice cream for all the kids. Want to ride with me", Davis asked as he looked at Darcy. Her heart fluttered. How much had he just heard? Should she even care? She stood up and kissed Kim on the forehead. The older lady winked at her and waved her away.

"Sure, I'll ride with you."

Once they were in the car Darcy looked shyly at Davis and said, "Thank you for last night. It meant a lot to me."

Davis smiled and said, "Me too."

There was something she had wanted to say but she wasn't sure if it would come out if she paused so she just blurted it out. "Would you like to stay with me tonight? I mean *really* stay with me tonight?"

Davis raised an eyebrow. "I would love to if that's what you want."

She blinked rapidly. "It is. I'm sure of it so can we say seven o'clock again?"

Davis chuckled. "Seven o'clock it is."

They drove into town and all through the ride she wondered if she was wrong not to tell him what his brother had done earlier that day. She decided it would only cause problems so she chose not to say anything. What his little brother thinks is totally irrelevant.

When they returned, Davis carried in the ice cream and she followed him in the door. She noticed Michelle reading a magazine in the front room so she stopped. "We haven't been formally introduced. My name is Darcy Scott. You're Michelle, right?"

The look on Michelle's face was almost as frightening as if she had seen a ghost. "Yes, I know who you are. I don't think it's a good idea if you and I talk. I'm very sorry. It's nothing personal."

With that being said, Michelle laid down her magazine and walked out the front door. Darcy wasn't angry. Yes, she was shocked but not angry. She realized that Michelle was only doing what she was told. Jonah had obviously forbidden Michelle from speaking to Darcy. Poor woman. How horrible it must be to have a tyrant for a husband.

Darcy went into the kitchen and helped dish out ice cream to all the kids. Thankfully Jonah had claimed he had some business in town and he had left earlier. Darcy was happy that she didn't have to face him for the rest of the day. It seemed that no amount of bestselling book deals could make her any less of a stranger to Jonah.

When Darcy was ready to head back to the hotel she bid everyone goodbye and gave Davis a conspirators' nod. He knew what she meant. Seven o'clock sharp. She was reminding him. This time it was really happening. No going back. She knew now more than ever that her future was not with Michael. It had only been four days but in those four days, she had found what she had been looking for all her life.

Chapter 20

Jonah jerked the sheet off the young lady lying next to him. "Damn it Katie, I don't come out here every other weekend for you to cover your naked body up! You're mine until at least midnight. That means I can look at all of you the entire time."

Katie had been hooking up with her ex-brother-in-law Jonah for these secret meetings for quite a long time. "It's a shame that you come all this way to see me but only see your mom every blue moon. She may not be my mother-in-law anymore but she's still a good woman. You're too hard on her," Katie exclaimed while trying to recover herself against his wishes.

"Mom sees me enough. She doesn't need me anyway. She has your perfect ex-husband to do her bidding. He's always been the only son she ever needed. Dad was the same way. Davis this and Davis that. It was nauseating."

Katie cut her eyes at Jonah. "Don't start on me about Davis. He wasn't half the man in bed that you are. Too bad you had to go and knock up that weak little twit you're married to or it could've been me and you."

Jonah snapped his head around and made direct eye contact as he spoke slowly. "It would never have been me and you. That twit has more class than you ever will and she knows her place. She speaks when spoken to. She isn't like you. You're just a loud mouth bitch. As a matter of fact, you're just lucky that I have a soft spot for whores. It must run in the family." Jonah threw back his head and started laughing.

Katie just smiled. He could call her all the names he wanted but she knew he needed her as much as she needed him. Jonah had provided a steady source of income for Katie and had done so even before she divorced Davis. Her ex-husband never knew that his little brother was doing the job that he never could.

On the other hand, Jonah came to her like clockwork because she provided him with the spunk, excitement, and passion he didn't get at home. It was a win-win situation.

Jonah had only married Michelle because he got drunk one night, slept with her, and got her pregnant. He didn't even remember that night very well but as soon as a child came into the picture, there was no going back. It helped Michelle's cause immensely that her father was the president of a very well-known bank. 'It is what it is,' as they say. At this late date it didn't matter how they got where they were. They were here now.

Jonah rolled on his side and ran his index finger down the side of Katie's right breast. "I have a proposition for you my sweet. I think my brother fancies himself in love. He's seeing someone new. Someone that I would like to see sent back to where she came from. I could make it worth your time to show up tomorrow evening at the ranch. Tell Davis you love him; miss him, whatever you have to say to make him dump his new fling. Then of course, once she's gone, you can get rid of him again and we will go back to life as usual."

Jonah winked at her. She scratched her ear, thought a minute, and said, "How much does it pay?"

He knew he had her at that point. Katie was the most materialistic tramp known to man. She would do anything for the right price. The two of them spent the next hour discussing how much it would cost to destroy Davis' life again.

Chapter 21

Michael had packed the last of his bags into the taxi. He was doing a last minute inventory.   Plane ticket-check. Baggage-check. Obscenely expensive engagement ring-check.

Michael was so nervous. He wanted to surprise Darcy and make this night something she would remember for the rest of her life.

He arrived at the airport with only a short time to spare, checked his bags, and boarded. He decided that his plan included going to the hotel first. If she wasn't there, he would wait. The flight lasted several hours. With every mile he traveled, he became increasingly more nervous. This was going to be the start of a new life for the two of them.

Once Michael landed he tracked down the baggage claim, picked up his suitcase, and went to hail a taxi. He had no need to rent a car. Darce already had one and all he needed was the ride to the hotel. They would use her rental car for the duration of the time they were here.

Michael enjoyed the scenery during the ride to her hotel. He could see why she loved the place. It was beautiful here. Maybe they could discuss buying a home here and relocating. Darcy could write in any state and he could move jobs if needed. Whatever made his future wife the happiest. He tried to make small talk with the driver the whole ride. When they reached their destination he paid the fare and the driver smiled and congratulated him.

Michael carried his suitcase and carry-on bag into the lobby. A valet approached him and asked if he could help with his bags. Michael pulled out a twenty dollar bill and asked the boy if there was anywhere he could leave his luggage safely for about thirty minutes. The young valet with the name tag that read Chip was only too happy to help out after he found out the story of why Michael was here.

"So, uh, Chip. You think you can point me to the elevator," he asked. "My soon to be wife is in room 232."

Chip lead the way and as Michael stepped onto the elevator the boy winked at him and said, "Good luck sir."

This really felt good. The most important decision of his life and he couldn't get to her fast enough. It was the best when you knew you had the right person. No more guessing.

Michael looked at his watch. "7:45," he said to himself. The doors in front of him opened. He stepped off the elevator and took a right.

His heart was pounding in his ears as he reached into his pocket and brought out the one and a half carat diamond engagement ring. He wanted to have it in hand when she opened the door.

"You can do this Mike. This is just Darce. The woman you are going to spend your life with. You won't blow it. She will be so happy. Just do it. Make that move." he thought to himself silently.

Chapter 22

Davis had shown up promptly at seven o'clock. Darcy knew what she wanted tonight and it wasn't dinner and late night TV. She answered the door wearing a silk nightgown in a smooth shade of pale yellow. It had small spaghetti straps and ended mid-calf.

Davis was pleasantly shocked to see her so ready to go so fast. His eyes were full of appreciation as he entered the room, closing the door behind him. "Darcy, you look amazing. I feel overdressed for the occasion," he joked. Although he only had on jeans and a polo shirt, that seemed overdressed compared to the sight in front of the open door.

She smiled coyly and replied, "Don't worry. You won't be overdressed for long."

She reached for his hand and pulled him close. Darcy leaned in slowly and fluidly brushed her lips across his. He groaned. He was sure that this woman was going to be the death of him if he didn't touch her soon. Davis pulled away and began to slowly take off his jacket. He draped it over the chair. He wanted to take his time and make this night last forever. He slipped off his shoes as she sat on the side of the bed watching him carefully. All she could think was how glorious this man looked undressing in front of her.

It seemed to take forever for him to come over to her. He wore only his pants and those were unbuttoned. He leaned over her until she reclined back onto the bed. His strong arms lowered himself on top of her. As he leaned in to put his lips on hers, there was a knock at the door. Davis froze. Darcy looked puzzled. "It must be housekeeping. I'll just go see what they need," she said. What a terrible time to bring clean linens. Didn't these people understand privacy?

Davis rolled over so that she could get up off the bed. "It's ok. We can pick up where we left off. We have all night. Put the 'do not disturb' sign out when they leave," he said.

She laughed and grabbed her robe. She turned the handle on the door and kneeling in front of her with an enormous diamond ring in his hand was Michael.

Panic flooded Darcy and not only glued her feet to the floor but froze her tongue as well. He had a huge smile on his face as he said, "Darce, you are my world. Marry me and make me the happiest man ever."

She was a statue of fear. This was surely karma extracting revenge upon her soul.

Michael thought it was happy shock until he looked past Darcy and watched a tall dark haired man walk up behind his girlfriend. The man was shirtless and his pants were unbuttoned. The strange man appeared to be as shocked as Michael felt.

Oh please let this be a nightmare, Darcy thought.

Michael slowly got up off his knee to stand straight. He cupped his hand around the diamond ring he was displaying only moments before.

"Darce, please tell me who this is and that this isn't what it looks like," Michael muttered still watching the dark haired man closely.

Darcy dropped her head and opened her mouth but nothing came out.

Michael took two steps back, pivoted, and fled. The ring had been dropped to the floor as Michael had escaped.

"Michael please wait!" Darcy screamed.

By the time she could will her legs to move, Michael was long gone. Her only option was to turn and face Davis.

She couldn't imagine what he must be thinking. Davis was sitting in the chair by the window with his head in his hands.

"Davis, I can explain. Please just hear me out," Darcy pleaded.

He stood up and put his shirt and shoes on.

"You don't owe me any explanation. This was a mistake," he said.

Before she could respond, Davis was out the door and gone. The door slowly closed on the silent spring hinges leaving Darcy standing alone in her room.

Chapter 23

Davis didn't get out of bed the next day until around lunch time. He didn't even have the desire to get up at all but he knew that his mother would worry if he didn't. He took a shower and dressed. As he walked down the hallway he ran head on into his brother.

"Hey bro. Have a long night?" Jonah asked.

"I'm not in the mood for you today Jonah. Leave me alone," Davis growled.

Jonah threw his hands up in mock surrender. "Sorrrrry."

Davis stomped off to the porch and sat down in a rocker. How could she do this to him? She had a boyfriend and didn't say anything. How could he be so stupid to think he might fall for a wonderful girl? Darcy was a liar and liars had no place in his life anymore. He had to move on. He would just make sure that he wasn't here for the next two days that Darcy had left on her visit. If she had a decent bone in her body she would not come back. Was he destined to fall for women who are cheaters? He felt so betrayed, so disgusted.

He rose out of the chair to go inside. He was going to pack a bag and tell his mother he had last minute, out of town business. A hotel room would be a great place to hide, preferably a hotel
on the opposite side of town as Darcy's.

As Davis started to open the screen door to go in, he heard a car coming down the driveway. He turned and watched a small black car pull up. It wasn't Darcy but he couldn't recognize who it was right away. When the person climbed out of the car he immediately knew her. The last couple of years had changed nothing.

Katie still looked like she did the day she signed the divorce papers. What in the world could she possibly want now, he thought. She sure picked a hell of a day to reappear no matter what the reason. One cheater in twenty four hours was all he could stand. Katie slung her purse over her shoulder and started towards the front porch where he stood. "What can we do for you Katie," Davis asked.

She smiled that all American cheerleader smile she was famous for and said, "I actually thought that maybe you and I could talk for a few minutes. If that's alright with you."

He paused and eyed her suspiciously. This woman had caused him nothing but pain. What could they possibly have to say to each other now? Davis opened the screen door and motioned for her to enter. Another bad decision couldn't hurt, why not invite her in? She followed him into the front room which was currently unoccupied. That was a miracle. It was hard to find a room in the Boyden house that wasn't occupied by at least one person.

He sat on the chair closest to the door. She sat on the sofa. Katie put her purse down, folded her hands, and began to talk.

"Davis, I've been thinking a lot about what happened with our marriage. I was so terribly wrong. You are the only man I have ever loved. I want us to try to become friends and hopefully I can redeem myself enough to have you back in my life one day. I know you must still love me because two people who love one another as much as we do never lose that love. I know this is probably a shock but please consider it before you just say no. I can't live without you anymore baby."

This was the absolute last thing that Davis ever expected her to come here and say. He thought maybe she needed money or free legal work or anything other than his love. He stalled for a few moments before he finally answered her plea. "Katie, what you did to me destroyed my life. You hurt me worse than anyone ever has. Yes, I do still love you and always will. That happens to be my curse in life. I don't know how to rebuild a relationship with you or if I even want to but I will at least try to be your friend."

Katie wiped a tear out of the corner of her eye and smiled. "Thank you. You don't know how much this means to me. I promise we will start over. If friends are all we can be right now then I will take it. I can only pray you will change your mind when you see how I've changed," Katie said. She rose and came over to Davis. She leaned down and kissed him softly on the cheek.

"Would you like to stay for dinner?" Davis asked her.

"Yes, I think I would," she replied.

Darcy had spent the better part of the night crying on the floor. She couldn't believe what had just happened. Michael hadn't even hinted that he would come here. He must be thinking that she is the most terrible person alive. She had never meant to hurt Michael and she sure hadn't meant to hurt Davis. Now Davis believed her to be a liar and a tramp. Jonah was right. It was over.

Darcy had called Michael's cell phone over and over since almost an hour after the bomb dropped. He had finally turned it off. Darcy knew this because now it wouldn't even ring; it just went straight to his voice mail. She was even too ashamed to leave a message. She decided that she had no other choice but to go to the ranch and apologize to Davis and try to explain. If he still had no inclination to see or talk to her she would say her goodbyes, pack up, and head back to New York. She tried to pull herself together. It was especially hard to make her red and puffy eyes diminish. The entire world could look at this woman and know she had been crying for quite a while.

Darcy pulled her long dark hair into a ponytail, threw on jeans and a tee-shirt, and left the hotel. She tried Michael's cell phone a couple more times and still nothing. Darcy pulled up at the ranch around five o'clock in the evening. She noticed there was a strange car parked in the yard. She walked around the house to the kitchen door and heard laughter coming from inside. As she opened the door she saw Davis standing next to a very attractive young lady. She had her hand on his shoulder in a way that suggested they knew one another quite well. Whatever they were talking about was enough to make Davis laugh so hard he was bent over. Darcy pushed the door open further and it made a high pitched squeaking noise. The two turned around to see who was coming in. When Davis saw Darcy he looked at Katie and said, "Excuse me for a moment. I need to go make a call." He turned and walked out without looking back.

Darcy suddenly felt very awkward. Katie knew instinctively who this woman was. She didn't know her name but she knew by the look on Davis' face that she was the one. Katie smiled big and extended her hand. "Hi, I'm Katie. Davis' wife, well, I mean, ex-wife. You are?"

Darcy was a bit choked up. She cleared her throat and accepted the girl's hand shake. "I'm Darcy Scott. I used to live here when I was a child in the foster system. I'm just in town visiting Kim."

Katie jumped on that comment as quickly as she could, "Oh so you and Davis are like brother and sister. How sweet. It's so nice to meet you. Will you be staying for dinner with us? Davis and I are spending the day together. We're working on rebuilding our marriage. I can't help but tell everyone because I'm so excited. Isn't that wonderful? He still loves me after all the mistakes I made."

Darcy didn't know what to say. She didn't belong here and she needed to get out as soon as she could. Nothing short of fleeing the property would make her breathe any better right now. "I was...I was...just looking for Kim to tell her that I'm heading out to New York tonight. Please tell her for me. It was nice to meet you. Good luck with your marriage. I wish you all the best," Darcy said as she started to tremble.

She didn't give Katie time to say anything before she turned and walked back out the way she came in. Katie had a huge smile on her face because she knew that she was much closer to her payment for a job well done. All she had to do now was put up with that sniveling cry baby Davis for another day or two then she could dump him and go back to her life. Damn Jonah for making her work so hard for her money. She didn't mind too much. Payback for being divorced with nothing sounded sweet, now that she thought about it.

Katie went in search of Davis and found him coming out of his bedroom. "Honey, that nice girl that came to see your mom told me to tell your mom that she was going back to New York tonight. She seems nice, is she a friend of yours?" Katie asked innocently.

"No, not a friend. Just someone who used to live her through the system. I barely remembered her when she showed up a couple of days ago."

Kim was quite surprised to see Katie here with her son. Actually disturbed was a better word. Kim could usually find the good in most people but this girl wasn't one of them. She knew how horrible she had treated Davis and she didn't want to see her do it again. She was also wondering what had happened to make Darcy go back to New York sooner than planned. Something was going on and Kim knew it wasn't good.

Jonah and his wife had declined dinner at the house on this night. Jonah decided it was best if he wasn't there to interfere with Katie's plan. She always worked better solo. Katie had called Jonah from her cell to let him know about her confrontation with Darcy and how she was going to be having dinner at the ranch. The plan was to meet after she left his mom's for Jonah to give her the payment and of course the always fun romp in the bed. They would meet at her place and he would tell Michelle he had to go out for a while. She wouldn't wonder. She never did. Michelle was a woman who knew how to keep her nose out of her man's business. He liked that. When Katie left the ranch she would call Jonah and he would make his excuses to his wife and head to her house.

Davis tried to remove Darcy from his thoughts all throughout the meal. Katie was being so polite to him and the conversation was light. He knew his mother was suspicious but she didn't seem to mind Katie's presence all that much. Katie told Davis all about where she was living now, about how her job at the salon was going, and all about her family. Davis had to admit it was nice to catch up on each other's lives. He guessed that he probably hadn't really gotten over her. Maybe she really had seen the light and wanted to have a real family. It wasn't too late to start over and they were still young enough to have the kids he always wanted. These were just thoughts he was bouncing around inside his head. He decided to play it by ear and let his heart lead him. The time for logical thinking was over. Darcy was logical and look what that got him. Maybe everyone deserves a second chance. The only question was, which one would get the second chance? He had never even let Darcy explain herself. Too bad, it was over. His place was not with Darcy but maybe it always was with Katie.

When Katie got ready to say her goodbyes she thanked her ex-mother-in-law for a lovely dinner and gave her a hug. Kim returned the affection and bid her goodnight as she cleaned off the table and prepared to start washing dishes. Davis could see the tension in his mother's body language as he turned away to walk his ex-wife to the door. "Thank you for staying with us for dinner. I had a nice time," he told her.

"You're very welcome. I had fun. If you're in town tomorrow please stop by the salon and maybe we can go to lunch," she replied.

He smiled at her faintly and said, "I think I just might do that." She nodded slightly and walked down the steps to her car. She waved goodbye as she got in and drove off. He stood staring after her for a while until her car was long gone. As he walked into the house, his mother was waiting for him. Davis stopped in front of her.

"Son, you are a grown man and I don't want to stick my nose where it doesn't belong but I worry about you. What in the world are you doing with that girl again? What happened with Darcy?"

Davis held his hand up between them as if to fend off any more questions.

"Mom, I know you're worried but please don't start with me. Darcy and I were just friends. Katie stopped by just to talk and I invited her to eat with us. Is that so wrong? She just made some mistakes and now she's seeing what she did wrong. You should be able to appreciate that. I actually applaud her for having the nerve to come admit she screwed up."

Kim looked into his eyes for a few moments and walked away. She knew that everyone had to make their own choices and if her son was set on taking this path, there was nothing she could do. As bad as she knew this choice was, she was helpless to stop it from happening. No good ever came from that woman.

Chapter 24

Davis went out onto the porch and sat for almost an hour just thinking about all that had happened in the last few days. For Davis Boyden, marriage vows meant something and if there was a chance he could make good on those vows, he would. Deep down he knew he didn't feel the same for Katie as he used to but it seemed that he would never feel that way again. He had felt that way for Darcy, or at least he thought he did, but he couldn't think of that right now.

He decided that he needed to talk to Katie and be sure of her intentions before this continued any further. He went into the house and grabbed his coat. He was intent on going over to Katie's house to talk with her. He couldn't wait. If he didn't go, he knew he wouldn't sleep a wink all night.

Davis drove up Katie's street and parked in her driveway. It was late but if he had to wake her up to hash this out, so be it. He got out of the car and went to the front door and knocked. Somewhere in the distance he heard a dog barking. It took a few minutes but he finally heard footsteps coming down the hallway. The porch light came on and the door swung open. Katie was standing in front of him in a flimsy pink robe. Her eyes flew open wide when she realized who was on her doorstep. She looked very shocked to see her ex-husband.

"Davis, is something wrong? What are you doing here?"

He pushed his way into the house past her.

"I really needed to talk to you. It couldn't wait. You said you want to start over and I need to know that you're serious before this goes any further."

Katie appeared to be blocking him from entering the house any further. She was stammering as she assured

Davis that she did want to begin again and that as soon as morning came they would talk about it more. He wondered why she seemed to be shaking and suddenly felt bad for waking her at such a late hour. That was a selfish thing to do. His crazy mind was getting the best of him today.

"Katie, I'm sorry I woke you. I'm just confused and more than a little nervous. I guess I just had to talk to you one last time. I won't keep you any longer. Have a nice sleep and I will see you in the morning."

Davis started to say goodbye with a kiss on the cheek when he heard a toilet flush in the back of the house. He stopped and whipped around toward the hallway.

"Who's here with you Katie?"

She began to stutter something he couldn't quite understand. He bolted through her arm's length barrier, stomping back through the hallway. Katie was running behind him trying to grab his arm. "Davis, Davis, please wait. It's a friend from work. I'm letting her use my room. She got kicked out. Please wait!"

Davis flung the bedroom door open and coming out of the bathroom naked as the day he was born was Jonah. Davis stumbled back a few feet. Blackness flooded his eye sight and a loud ringing blasted into his ears. The sight of his brother, his married brother, in his ex-wife's bed was more than he could bear.

Jonah stood completely still staring at Davis like he had never seen him before. It occurred to Jonah that his brother may just kill him right here in his girlfriend's house. Jonah never expected him to show up like this. His plan had backfired and now there would be hell to pay.

Davis turned to Katie who was already starting to panic. She appeared to be hyperventilating. "Do not ever show your face around me again. You disgust me. To think that I ever loved you makes me sick!" he said as he thrust his finger in her face.

He turned toward Jonah who seemed to be trying to

put his pants on as quickly as possible. "I used to love you no matter how big of a bastard you were but no more! I don't know how to deal with you yet because I happen to care about our family but you can be sure to know that you WILL be dealt with. Both of you can go to HELL!" He pushed Katie out of the way and stormed out the front.

Chapter 25

Darcy had returned home to New York only to find Michael's key to her apartment lying on her kitchen counter. Seeing that little piece of metal lying there so lonely made her realize that this was truly the end. She had stopped attempting to contact him. It was obvious that he wanted nothing more to do with her. She just wanted him to know what had happened and that she was willing to take full responsibility for the situation so she sat down and wrote him a letter. She tried to explain the best she could and in the end, she promised him she would never contact him again.

The past week had turned out to be the worst she had encountered in a very long time. She had lost two good men at one time. It must've been for the best because Davis had turned to his ex-wife for support and comfort. She seemed to be a lovely girl and Darcy would have loved to say that she hoped it worked out for them but she just couldn't. She was still very much wounded that she had lost her chance with Davis. She thought it should've been her with Davis and not Katie. How could one person screw up so much in such a short time? If someone could answer that, she would feel so much better. There was nothing more to do but try to pick up the pieces of her life and move on. It wouldn't be easy but it was necessary.

Davis had driven around all night long trying to decide what needed to be done about Jonah. "How in the hell am I going to tell Michelle? How can I not tell her?" He slammed his hands on the steering wheel in frustration. What a week! To lose a new love, an old love, and a brother all in one week was too much for anyone to take. The strong sense of right and wrong in Davis made him see that he had no choice but to 'spill the beans' as they say. Maybe it was his raising or maybe it was because he was an officer of the court, either way, he couldn't condone harboring a lie; especially to his family.

When he finally drove into the yard, the sun was up and activity was already beginning to start at the house. He noticed Jonah's car was not in the driveway. Coward! Can't even face the people he has hurt. Kim met Davis at the front door.

"Son, where have you been? I was so worried when I saw you didn't come home last night. If you're going to stay with Katie you should've called so I didn't worry."

He dropped his head. "Mom, I didn't stay with Katie. I need to talk with Michelle. Where is she?"

Kim looked at her son quizzically. She could tell when there was something major going
on. "She's in the kitchen with the baby."

He nodded absently. "Can you take the baby and ask her to come into the den and talk with me please?"

Now she knew there was something wrong. Jonah hadn't come home last night either and now Davis wanted to talk to Michelle. Kim could feel the dark cloud moving in.

Davis was sitting on the couch when Michelle entered the room. "You wanted to talk to me in private?"

He motioned for her to sit down across from him. His other hand was cradling his forehead. Michelle had never seen her brother-in-law look so worried. As his hand came down from his face he started to speak.

"Michelle, this is very hard for me to talk about so you have to bear with me. Let me finish before you say anything. I will tell you everything I can. After Katie left last night I did a lot of thinking and I decided to go to her house. I wanted to talk to her about where we stood with our situation. I got to her house and it appeared that she wasn't alone. I heard someone in her bedroom. I went to see who it was. When I opened the door I found a naked man in her room...it was Jonah. I lost my head and said a lot of cruel things to both of them and left. I've been riding around all night trying to decide how to tell you the truth. I'm so sorry."

Michelle looked as if all the color had drained out of her face. She slowly started to shake her head from side to side. It was the action of someone who was about to protest. "If this is some kind of joke, I'm not laughing. Jonah was out with a business acquaintance. He told me he might stay over at the client's house to keep from disturbing us coming in the hotel room so late. You're mistaken."

Her tone was matter of fact. She was sure this was just a mistake and it would all be cleared up immediately. Jonah had this woman deluded worse than anyone knew.

"No, Michelle. It was not a mistake. I spoke to him. I watched him put his pants back on. Your husband is sleeping with my ex-wife. You're a good woman and you don't deserve the way he treats you. I can't tell you what to do with your marriage but I can tell you that Jonah is unfaithful. Do with it what you will."

"I think I can tell you what to do with it! Stop telling my wife lies!" Jonah bellowed from the open doorway.

Davis jumped to his feet. "No one's telling any lies but you, you low life, son of a…"

"Boys! Please NO!" Michelle screamed.

Kim came running into the room breathless.

"Mom, stay out of this. It's between me and Davis," Jonah barked.

"No, it's between all of us. So what was your plan little brother? You and your tramp decide that I hadn't been hurt enough so you would send her back to me to offer up another helping? Do you really hate me that much?"

Jonah was red in the face and starting to ball up his fists. "What do you care about anyone? Davis the perfect son, perfect husband, blah blah blah! You're just mad because someone ran off your orphan girlfriend so you have to make up lies to make everyone else miserable!"

Kim and Michelle both were looking back and forth between the two brothers wondering who was going to swing the first punch.

"I see now," Davis said. "You were pissed because I found someone to fall in love with that was a great person who could make me happy. You never wanted anything good for me our whole lives!"

Jonah was turning a shade of red that seemed to be purple. He was so angry at that point that he decided he had nothing left to lose. Michelle was going to hear it all thanks to his brother so why not go ahead and say everything he was holding inside.

"You think you're so smart don't you? Well guess what big brother, you're nothing but a fool. I had Katie come back to run Darcy off. You stole all the glory all my life! I'll be damned if I'm going to let you be happy the rest of yours. I had your hot little wife throughout your whole marriage. That's right! We did it right under your nose and you were too stupid to see it. So when I sent her over here to run off your new girlfriend you fell hook, line, and sinker. Now who's so smart?"

Michelle sucked in her breath and sank to the floor. Kim knelt down beside her trying to revive her daughter-in-law. She appeared to be silently weeping while she rubbed Michelle's forehead.

Davis could hardly contain himself. He drew back and let go. His fist made contact with Jonah's nose and you could hear the crack. Blood flew in all directions. Jonah grabbed his face and doubled over.

Kim jumped up and stood iron straight. She had had enough. In all her years of trying to live the life of a good woman, she never thought she would be here in this moment in her own house. "ENOUGH! Stop it, both of you. I will not tolerate this in my home. Jonah, get your things and leave now. You have let your whole family down. I thought I raised you better than that but obviously

I failed. Davis, you need to leave until you can calm down. Someone has to take care of Michelle, obviously you two aren't capable of that right now. Please leave my house!"

Both men had stopped fighting to listen to their mother. Jonah was using his shirt to stop the heavy flow of blood coming from his nose.

Davis turned and walked out the door without a word. Jonah was about to do the same when suddenly Michelle, who had managed to sit up on the floor, spoke to him.

"Jonah, before you go, know this; your son and I will not be coming home. I will be filing for divorce first thing Monday morning. I know a great attorney who will take my case." Jonah shot her an angry look and left.

Chapter 26

The weeks that followed were hard on everyone. Michelle had sent someone for her and A.J.'s belongings and stayed on at Kim's house. She had appealed to Davis for legal help. He had filed her divorce papers and acted as her attorney, free of charge naturally.

Jonah had stayed at their marital home but no one had seen him. He didn't even show up for the divorce hearing. Michelle got the spousal and child support she requested. She said she didn't want the house; she would start over somewhere that didn't have all the memories.

Kim had tried to contact her son and even his cell phone had been disconnected. Davis had no need to find Jonah. He cared to never see him or Katie ever again. It only bothered him that his brother cared so little for his son. He hadn't seen A.J. since the day the fight happened and he was asked to leave. Rumors were going around town that Katie had quit her job at the salon and left the area. Good riddance to bad rubbish, Davis thought.

He threw himself into his work harder than ever and occasionally he caught himself wondering where Darcy was and what she was doing. He knew that no matter what happened it didn't excuse what she did when she lied to him about that other man.

Poor sap. He must've taken it really hard. For all Davis knew, she could've reconciled with the guy. Who knows?

Darcy had finished her fourth book. It was titled 'Blind Rage.' It had made a big hit with readers. All the critics were raving about what a talented and unique writer she was. It had been almost eight months since the catastrophe at the ranch happened. It still saddened her to think of how it all went down. Too much drama. She brought it on herself and now she was learning how to be alone.

The few friends she had in her life had given up on her when they realized she just wasn't ever going to go out and socialize. Finally the calls stopped coming. The invitations to movies and dinners ceased. Darcy didn't care. She knew that if she just stayed away from everyone she wouldn't chance hurting someone else.

Most of her time was spent writing anyway. Work seemed to be her only reliable companion. Darcy was lying on her couch one Monday thinking about how she dreaded going to the supermarket when someone knocked on her door. Surprised that she would have a visitor she sat up and swung her legs off the furniture.

"I'm coming," she yelled. As she plodded on her bare feet towards the door, she wondered who could possibly be coming to see her. Darcy flipped the door lock and the latch. No matter what neighborhood you lived in it was still necessary to have two locks or more in New York. She cracked open the door and at first she didn't recognize him.

The man in front of her doorway had shaggy, unkempt dark hair that looked as if it hadn't seen a washing in weeks. His tee-shirt was rumpled and stained, as were his jeans. If it hadn't been for the look in his eyes, she wouldn't have known that it was Jonah Boyden. His appearance made her open the door further, against her better judgment.

"Jonah, what are you doing here? How did you find me and why do you look like you do?" Her eyes squinted against the hallway lighting.

His eyes were glassy in a strange way. Maybe it was lack of sleep. She couldn't quite put her finger on it.

"Darcy, I came to apologize for my behavior last time we saw each other. Can I please come in?"

She was puzzled. Why would someone who never liked her come all this way to apologize for something that didn't matter now anyway? Something was wrong with this situation, she could feel it in her bones.

"You have nothing to apologize for Jonah. Thank you for coming but I really can't have guests right now."

Darcy tried to close the door but he put his hand on it to hold it open.

"Please, just give me five minutes of your time," he pleaded. The hand that held the door was trembling slightly and part of her felt a twinge of sympathy for this obviously broken man. Whatever had happened to this person since she had last seen him must have been rough.

She sighed heavily and decided she could at least hear him out. She released the door handle and let it swing open.

"Come on in."

Darcy turned to walk into the living room with Jonah following behind her.

She heard the door click closed but before she could reach the sofa she felt a blinding pain shoot through her head like an explosion. Everything went black.

Chapter 27

Kim had cried herself to sleep every night for months since her family fell apart. It seemed that overnight everyone just exploded. Michelle and the baby were still with her in the house but she hadn't laid eyes on Jonah in months. The divorce had gone through and he hadn't even visited with A.J. The child missed his father dreadfully. Michelle refused to even discuss it. She secured a job at her father's bank and seemed to be doing much better. She could finally come out of her shell without anyone to hold her back.

One Saturday evening, Kim had her grandson and two of her foster children in the front yard building stick forts when a car pulled through the open gate. It was an older model Dodge she had never seen before. The car parked in the gravel area to the side of the porch. Kim stood to her feet and dusted her trousers off. The children continued to play, oblivious to the new arrival.

The man who stepped out wasn't very tall, maybe five nine or so. His once dark hair had gotten silver around the edges. At first Kim couldn't recognize him but once he faced her fully she knew exactly who this man was.

"Carmen! Please come watch the younger children while I speak to my guest."

The thirteen year-old Carmen came swiftly out the front door to do as she was told.

The man swaggered over to the steps to meet Kim. He extended his hand towards her.

"Hello Mrs. Boyden. It's a pleasure to see you after all these years."

"We shouldn't have this talk outside. Please follow me into the house."

The man nodded as if he understood completely and followed her up the steps and into the house. She led him to the kitchen area and motioned for him to take a seat.

"I would ask you if you would like something to drink but I assume that by your being here, there must be a much larger reason for you to show your face. Even after all these years you know that it's still illegal for you to break our contract. You shouldn't be here."

"I do know that but I'm only here because I need your help. I made a huge mistake and I believe the wrong person may pay for it. Kim, you're the only one who can help me."

The man had the desperation of a thousand lifetimes in his voice. Kim raised her hand to rub her forehead. Nothing this man had to say could be good and she knew it. She actually dreaded hearing what was coming next.

"Well, let's hear it Marco. What have you done now?"

Marco Bennett was fifteen years-old when he met Marsha Scott. She was the prettiest girl in his whole class but she never spoke to him. She only giggled when she passed him. It took his entire freshman year to get her to go out with him but once she did, he was hooked. He would've done anything for Marsha and she knew it.

One night after a school football game, Marco was out behind the band room with Marsha and a few of her friends. The girls had a bottle of whiskey and were passing it around. Marco had refused each time Marsha asked him to drink but he was beginning to get tired of being the only one there who wasn't enjoying themselves.

It wasn't long before the two love birds were drinking and partying together as a couple. The drinking turned into a little coke and the blow turned into a lot of speed; all kinds. By junior year the two of them were more interested in getting high and wasted than graduating. Marsha's mom was threatening to throw her out and disown her. Marco's parents didn't have a clue as to what was going on.

The day that Marsha came to his house and told him

she was pregnant, the party stopped being so fun anymore. Marsha's mother had ordered her out of the house and she had nowhere to go except to him.

Marco did the only thing he knew to do. He told his mother about the baby and he married Marsha. The two of them dropped out of school to work but they still had to live with Marco's parents in the beginning. It wasn't ideal but it would have to do until the baby came. Marsha was not very happy at all about suddenly being expected to be clean and sober. They fought often when Marco would come home stoned and Marsha would scream.

"You are a bastard! It's your fault I'm pregnant and you're out there living it up while I suffer. I hate you!"

The screaming flowed from both sides and it wasn't long before Marco hated Marsha as much as she claimed to hate him.

The baby came on a freezing cold January night. The snow was so deep Marco was worried that his dad's old Ford wouldn't make it out of the driveway. Thank goodness it did and it also made the ten mile journey to the county hospital. The labor wasn't very long at all. It happened less than three hours after they arrived and had Marsha admitted. Marco was standing by his young wife when the doctor smiled up at him and said, "Congratulations, it's a boy."

Chapter 28

Kim braced herself to hear what Marco had to tell her. This man had shown up on her doorstep many years earlier in much the same way as today. She had seen the young man around and even knew his parents but when he knocked on her door thirty years ago, she never knew it would all turn out this way.

"Kim, please hear me out."

His declaration brought her out of the past and back to the impending problem at hand. She couldn't begin to imagine what he could've done that would have anything to do with her or her family.

"I'm listening Marco. Let's hear it. Stop stalling me."

"I've done a terrible thing."

"You've already told me that so now tell me what you're doing here."

"It was an accident. I ran into him in town and he looked so much like me at his age and I just wanted to know him. I stopped him and it just slipped out. At first he looked at me like a crazy homeless person until I asked about his sister."

Kim suddenly had the urge to faint. This couldn't be happening. Of all the things she and Albert had ever kept secret this would be the one to blow up in her face. The one secret that could destroy so much for her could already have come out. She held her hand to her mouth for a moment. As she began to fan her face with alarm, she said, "Please tell me you aren't talking about what I think you're talking about. You haven't seen that boy in thirty years. You don't even know if he knows about you or his sister but you thought it might be a great idea to just blurt it out on the street corner?" Her eyes rolled back into her head briefly.

"I know it was stupid and selfish but I always regretted

what we did. I just wanted to know
them. I swear. It was innocent, or at least I thought it
would be." Marco hung his head in shame.

"Tell me he ignored you. Tell me you didn't explain it
to him."

"I did. I thought he might tell me where his sister was
so I could make it up to both of them. I just wanted to let
them both know how sorry I was and how much I really
do love them both."

"What did he say to you when you told your story?"

"That's the problem Kim. He seemed to suddenly look
through me and he began to mumble something about
liars and ending it once and for all. Then he pushed past
me and ran off." Marco burst into tears. "I'm so sorry
Kim. I think I just made a worse mistake today than I did
years ago when I left."

"Of course you did, you idiot! You just told Jonah that
he isn't ours and to top it off you told him that Darcy
Scott is his sister. You have no idea what you have done.
Please leave my house, for good."

Marco begged for forgiveness as she ushered him out
the door. It didn't matter how sorry he was now. He had
ruined what took a lifetime to create. The man should
have never talked to Jonah. It was in the adoption
contract. How dare he destroy that boy all over again?
Kim fled to her bedroom with tears pouring as she went.
She never even noticed Davis standing in the hallway
listening to her conversation.

Chapter 29

Baby boy Jonah had been born just perfect. Marco was so happy to have a beautiful healthy boy. Marsha on the other hand was not impressed. She never bothered to have her name changed once they married so the tag on the little pink skinned boy said "Baby Boy Scott." Marsha hadn't spoken since the delivery. She didn't want to look at the baby or hold the baby. Marco was crushed. The baby had only been home a little over two weeks when Marco's mother approached him in private.

"Son, you need to face facts. That girl isn't mother material and that baby is suffering. She doesn't hold him or even talk to him. I cannot raise that child while she drinks herself into a daylight coma each day. You need to make a decision and do it soon. I know a family here in town that are good people and who would be willing to take the baby and raise him as their own, no questions asked. Think about it."

Marco knew that what his mother said was true. He had tried everything to get Marsha to bond with the boy. It was simple, she didn't want the baby. He even tried to talk to her about giving the baby away. Her response was always the same "Whatever you want."

Finally Marco asked his mother to have the couple come meet with them. The paperwork was filed and the baby became Jonah Boyden, youngest son of Kim and Albert Boyden and younger brother to three year old Davis. The only condition was that Marco or Marsha would be forever prohibited from contacting Jonah or revealing their true relationship. Jonah's first day being a Boyden came when he was only twelve weeks old.

The minute the baby was gone Marsha was transformed. She stayed out all day and night partying with friends. Marco worked long hours and found himself getting high more often. It dulled the pain of thinking about that little boy of his out there somewhere being held and cared for by strangers. He knew the Boydens would be good to the baby but it didn't make it hurt any less. That hurt somehow did not extend to his wife. Marsha was never better. A year after the baby had been sent away Marco's parents had enough of their daughter-in-law. They asked Marco to move out. He found a small upstairs apartment in town by the Maxwell Grocery store. It was really tiny but it was in his price range. He hoped that if he lived in town he could convince Marsha to stop her constant night life and get a job to pitch in on bills. That of course was not in her plan at all. The fighting between the couple was becoming epic.

"Do you think you could bring your sorry ass home occasionally and wash a dish or are you not interested in dishes that aren't covered in white powdered lines?"

"You can go to hell Marco. I don't see where it's any of your business what I do. Half the time you're either too drunk to care of too high to notice."

"The difference in me and you though is that I actually pay the bills to keep this shitty roof over your head. You know Marsha, you are the worst mistake I ever made."

No matter how many times he declared this to her she would simply laugh and walk out of the room. Most times she would just completely leave. He couldn't take it much longer. The desire to kill her had become so strong that he was afraid he was going to actually do it one day.

On their second anniversary he came home not expecting anyone to be there as usual but he was surprised. Marsha was home and she was sitting on the chair arm crying. Emotion was not something that Marsha made a habit of showing so something must be terribly wrong, he thought.

Marco threw his jacket over the back of the sofa.

"What's wrong with you? Someone die or did they

outlaw alcohol again?" He chuckled at his joke but when she didn't respond he realized there was something real to worry about.

"I said, what's wrong with you?"

Instead of speaking she simply tossed a long white plastic tube at him. It seemed to be some kind of home pregnancy test. There were two lines. Two lines were positive according to the indicator on the end of the item.

Oh no. This couldn't be happening again. They were hardly ever around one another enough to have sex. This was a nightmare. Marco sat down on the sofa and held his head in his hands. One time was all it takes to make a baby. Why weren't they more careful?

"Don't worry Marsha. It will work out, somehow." He assured her.

When he awoke the next morning for work he found her asleep on the sofa. That's where he would find her every day for the next twenty-eight weeks. The depression Marsha had suffered with the first child had been bad but nothing like what she was experiencing this time. Marco had to have a friend come by each day and force Marsha to get up and eat. She had to be coached to shower or even brush her hair. The stress had drove Marco into madness. He was a shell of his former self and when the day for labor finally arrived, he drove Marsha to the hospital. She was in a great deal of pain and labor lasted for hours on end. This would prove not to be as easy as it was when she had given birth to their son a few years before. Labor finally came to an end after fourteen hours when the doctor announced, "It is a girl."

Marco kissed his tiny daughter, filled out her paperwork to name her Darcy and left the hospital forever. The final gift to his baby girl was her name. Marsha had made it impossible to give the child his last name but she couldn't control what he chose to put as her first name. His grandmother had been named Darcy and he always knew if he had a daughter, she would be named after her.

He could not say goodbye to another child. Maybe with him gone Marsha would be forced to be a good mother. He could only pray.

Chapter 30

Jonah had managed to get Darcy to let him in. He didn't think the bitch would ever fall for it but she did. Once he got in and closed the door, he made his move. He quickly pulled the .38 revolver from the back of his jeans and slammed her in the back of the head with the butt. Down she dropped. Now that was a good feeling. It was all coming together for him.

He couldn't risk anyone hearing a gunshot right now, besides, she had been to blame for his life falling apart and he was going to teach her a slow and painful lesson. She was worth more to him alive than dead, at least for now. When the time was right he was going to enjoy her pain, sister or not.

When that man let the cat out of the bag it took him a while to recover from the shock but now he could see clearly. If he just made Darcy pay it would make his life better. It would make everyone's life better.

She went down like a sandbag on the floor. It seemed to take forever for him to pick her up and move her unconscious body down the back stairs, out into the alley, and into his parked car. Blood leaked from a cut behind her ear and made his hands slippery. He stuffed her in the trunk just in case he got pulled over or stopped at a red light. It would look really fishy if someone seen a slumped over woman in his back seat. Stupid bitch had already caused him enough problems to last a lifetime. He didn't need cops added to the list.

He drove across town to a most undesirable part of the city. The buildings were covered with graffiti and most of the shops were closed down and boarded up. He parked the car in back of a ratty old apartment building that looked like it should be scheduled for demolition any day now. The old metal door on the back was once green. You could see a faint chip of paint under the rust. Darcy was hauled out of the trunk and into the building by way of the back door. Jonah took pleasure in making sure her already bleeding head hit the trunk lid on her way out. Once inside the sparse apartment he dumped her body on a dingy green futon in the front room.

"What's all that damn noise?" Katie came out of the bedroom with a cigarette dangling from her lips wearing only a tank top and a pair of skimpy, purple cotton shorts.

Chapter 31

When Michelle divorced Jonah he quit his job and moved in with Katie. He had managed in the months since the divorce to sell everything he owned and deplete all his accounts. This did not please Katie but she didn't have many other options at this point.

Jonah and Katie had enjoyed quite the expensive drug habit for several months. The day finally came when the money and the assets ran out leaving both of them about forty pounds lighter, broke, and suffering from a strong addiction. The bottom really fell out when Marco ran into Jonah and told him the truth. Life had already dealt Jonah a strong dose of karma when the story of his real family found its way to him. The knowledge that he belonged to those people and not the ones who raised him was bad enough; but they expected him to live with the fact that the dirty little orphan whore was really his blood relation. No, he would not accept this. As a matter of fact, he must do something to rectify this whole ordeal. It was time to right some wrongs in his eyes.

Jonah refused to make any effort to talk to Michelle or even to see his son. He cut off all contact. The more cocaine and heroin he piled into his body the more fixated he became on Darcy Scott. He was convinced that if she had never come back he would still be with his wife and enjoying the good life instead of scrounging for his next high. He would still have a mother and a father who gave him life and loved him unconditionally. Now he had nothing and it was her fault. The only person who hadn't turned their back on him was Katie and she was simply along for the ride. He knew she didn't love him and never would. Katie didn't know how to love anyone but herself. She was a truly narcissistic creature.

Katie herself knew she didn't love Jonah, hell, she

wasn't even sure she liked him but so what. He was someone to stay with and help her get a fix when she needed it. Once you started spending too much time with drugs it had a way of taking everything you have and everything you didn't even know you had. One of the things it took from Katie was her job at the salon. People don't want to let someone cut their hair when she's too high to even stay awake. When the job was gone so was the house, the car and everything else Katie owed money on. So considering the circumstances she could care less what type of issues Jonah had. If he wanted to rant and rave about that Darcy girl it was okay with her. Of course, Katie's concern seemed to increase when she walked into a kidnapping scene. This was more than a little messed up, even for her.

"Jonah! What in the hell is she doing here? What have you done you moron?"

He had an evil smile on his face as he bent down in front of Darcy and began to secure duct tape on her arms and legs. She was still unconscious with blood matted in her dark hair. Katie rushed over to see if the girl was dead. Holy crap that idiot had finally went over the edge. She didn't need this shit. She really wondered why she didn't just find a different and less crazy meal ticket than Jonah. Katie bent over and touched the girl's throat to feel for a pulse. Found it. She appeared to be breathing, thank God. The dumbass hadn't killed her. They might have been better off if he had, she was thinking. If this girl wakes up, we're screwed. Now she was the one thinking off the wall thoughts. There had to be an explanation for this.

"I'm serious, Jonah. What is going on?"

When he had finished snugly taping Darcy he jumped up with an insane smile on his face. "Katie baby, don't you see? This is my chance to make the bitch pay and get us the money to get out of this dump. She's a hot shot author. Someone will pay to get her back and until then she's going to pay for each and every thing that I lost because of her butting into our lives." Katie was dumbfounded. How could he really believe this would work? Kidnapping another human being was strongly frowned upon by the police department. She could see them kicking in the door with guns blazing. This was not how she saw this week turning out for herself.

Jonah had no intention of sharing the truth with Katie. He wanted, no, he needed her to believe that this was a simple kidnapping for ransom because once he had the money he would enjoy himself by carving Darcy up really nice. Katie might do something to screw that up if she knew what was really going on. He couldn't take that chance. She had to be kept in the dark for now. Knowing the truth when no one else did made him feel like God. He knew the real connection between himself and everyone else but the best thing was that he held this life in his hands. He could choose to alter it at any time.

Darcy began to moan and stir. Her eyes fluttered. Her head felt like she had been hit by a train and her vision was blurred. Things were slowly coming into focus.

What had happened? She couldn't remember. As her vision began to clear further, she tried to rub her eyes and realized she couldn't move her hands. Her feet were frozen also. She looked up and saw what appeared to be a girl standing over her. The girl looked familiar but she couldn't place her. Suddenly she realized who she was with. It was Davis' ex-wife Katie. She must have died and surely slipped into the farthest corner of hell. This most definitely had to be a hallucination.

Katie looked rail thin with stringy long hair and her face was scarred from what looked to be terrible acne. This was not the beautiful girl she had met in the Boyden's kitchen that day. What had happened to her?

"What's going on? Where am I? How did I get here?" Darcy asked while still struggling to move her hands and feet.

Katie shook her head in disgust and walked away. Jonah appeared quickly by the side of the futon.

"You're here to make me some money bitch so stop your talking and listen to me. I lost my family because of you so someone's going to pay. I know you got a manager or a publisher that makes a lot of money on those books you write so I'm guessing they would be willing to pay top dollar to get their little cash cow back."

Darcy had no idea what he was talking about. Lost his family? What did that mean?

"Jonah, I don't know what I did, but really I am sorry if I caused anything bad to happen to anyone. We can work this out. I have money in the bank. I can pay you. If you'll just untie me we can come to an adult solution," Darcy tried to reason.

Jonah was furious. Every second she kept talking only made him angrier. Did she think he was stupid?

He drew back and hit her with the palm of his hand as hard as he could. You could hear the smack of skin hitting skin. Her head jerked backwards as blood sprayed from her nose.

"Lying whore! I'm not untying you. We're doing things my way. You're going to tell me the number to your richest friend and I'm going to call the number, hold the phone to your ear, and you're going to say what I tell you to and only what I tell you to. If you try to mention my name or Katie's I will shoot you while you're still on the phone."

Jonah pulled out his gun and Darcy started to shake. She didn't know why he was here or what had happened but it was obvious that Jonah had lost his mind. She knew she was in real danger and trying to reason with him would never work. She had no choice but to do as she was told and hope to find some way somehow to plan a getaway. The girl didn't seem too happy with her presence so maybe she was the ticket out of this filthy hole.

Darcy closed her eyes and said a silent prayer for help.

Katie was sitting at a small round kitchen table smoking a cigarette when she decided to speak up.

"Look, whatever you're going to do Jonah, just do it cause I'm hurting bad. We gotta go see Alberto soon or I'm gonna just die! I can't believe you're doing this crap now when you know we're out of our stash. Hurry the hell up you idiot."

"Shut up!" Jonah barked.

"Your fix can wait until after we make the ransom call. Besides, Alberto already said we owe him too much money. If we go back empty handed he'll rip my balls off. We gotta go somewhere else. Now be quiet and let me work!"

Katie flung her head back and growled her disapproval. Jonah pulled a cheap looking little cell phone out of his pocket.

"What's the number?"

Darcy's mind blanked. She couldn't think. It crossed her mind to call Michael but after all this time he probably wouldn't pay a dime for her release. He would most likely suggest they kill her. She didn't blame him. He wasn't her number one fan these days.

She finally told him the number to her publicist, Karen McCravy. Jonah dialed the number and held the phone to her ear. She could hear the ringing on the other end. Darcy was praying that Karen would answer a call from a number she didn't recognize. Her heart was beating in her ears as she prayed. Karen picked up on the third ring. Relief flooded her body.

Jonah shoved a paper in her face. On the paper he had written what he wanted her to say.   "Karen, this is Darcy. I have been kidnapped. They want one million dollars by Friday. You'll get a call notifying you of where to transfer the money. If you call the police they will kill me."

Jonah pulled the phone back and ended the call. Darcy could hear Karen crying when he took the phone away from her.

"Good job. Now, we have business in town. We're leaving you here but your accommodations won't be so nice. If you need to go to the rest room you better say so or else you can go in your pants."

Darcy shook her head no. Jonah came over with the tape roll, pulled off a large piece and put it over her mouth. (So much for trying to scream for help.) He put the phone and the door keys in his pocket. Katie pulled on a pair of faded jeans that were lying in the corner by the window and followed him out the door. The lock clicked loudly as they left her all alone and scared. She could hear Katie's voice as she faded away from the apartment.

She didn't know whether to cry or panic. This was like a nightmare that she was expecting to wake up from at any minute. To her fear and displeasure, that minute was not coming soon. Why in the world would Davis' ex-wife be here in New York with Davis' brother? None of this made sense. Where was Davis? Where was Jonah's wife Michelle?

Nothing was making sense to her. Not knowing was also making this situation like fighting an invisible foe. How do you defeat something you cannot see?

She attempted to roll slightly to her left to position herself in a more comfortable place. It would be necessary to conserve her energy for an opportunity to break free. It wasn't clear how or when but she knew she had to figure that out as she went.

Chapter 32

Karen McCravy had been Darcy's publicist since day one. Darcy was like a daughter to her. Karen was fifty-two and the age difference made no obstacle for their friendship. The two women were fast friends and cared for one another greatly. When the call came in that she had been kidnapped, Karen didn't know what to do. It took her a while to calm down long enough to use common sense. She knew that calling the police was the only choice. Darcy had warned her not to contact the authorities or they would kill her. However, Karen had watched too many movies where the people attempted to handle these things on their own. It almost never turned out good. She had to do the right thing and pray that it turned out to bring Darcy home safely. She would make it clear to the police that it had to be strictly confidential or else they said they would kill her. She couldn't risk Darcy's life.

Karen called the police station and was directed to a detective by the name of Charles Broman. She explained the situation in detail to Detective Broman and stressed how high profile this would be if it got out and how Darcy's life was at stake.

Broman explained that he would contact the FBI and they would arrive at her house in unmarked cars. He also explained that it would be necessary for them to go to Darcy's home and investigate. Broman assured her it would all be done with the utmost discretion.

"We understand your anxiety Ms. McCravy but I assure you that we have handled many kidnappings in the past and we are trained in these matters. You did the right thing by calling us. We will be at your home very soon."

Within the hour, Karen had detectives swarming her home and Darcy's. Officers at the Scott house were checking for trace evidence, fingerprints, phone messages, etc. In the interest of discretion the officers were wearing carpet cleaning uniforms. To the onlooker, it simply appeared that Darcy had hired a crew to spring clean her place. Kidnappers were rarely smart enough to see through such an obvious ruse.

The officers at Karen's house were installing a device to record and trace all her telephone calls. The only thing to do now was to wait.

Arthur Schmidt owned the building that Darcy's flat was in. He happened to be in the neighborhood looking over some of his properties when he noticed two large vans with the words "Carpet Cleaning Crew" parked along the street. It looked like they were all going in and out of Darcy's place. He decided he needed to go see if there were damages to the carpet or some major renovations going on. All of his tenants knew better than to remodel his locations without personal permission. She better hope that wasn't what was going on.

Darcy never gave him any problems. She had been with him for years on an ongoing lease. There had to be a major water leak or something of that nature happening. He parked in an adjacent parking area and let himself into the building. When he got past the foyer he saw about fifteen men moving around in and out of Darcy's apartment. The problem was that there seemed to be no equipment that you would normally have when cleaning carpets. He didn't hear any steamers running at all. There were no extension cords or hoses in sight.

Something was strange. He didn't see Darcy anywhere. Arthur rubbed his partially balding head and shouted, "Excuse me! Do you mind telling me what's going on?" What if these men were a group of robbers?

Several of the men turned around but no one volunteered an answer to Arthur's question. They merely looked at him as if he were a fly buzzing around their hats. Out of the group a large young man approached

Arthur.

"Who are you? Let's see some ID."

Arthur's eyebrows shot up.

"ID? I'm Arthur Schmidt and I own this building. Who are you and where is Miss Scott? I think it is you sir who needs to produce some identification."

Two of the men whispered out of ear shot. The big guy tugged at his earlobe and said, "I'm agent Fowler with the FBI. When's the last time you saw Miss Scott?"

Schmidt was shocked. FBI? Since when do the Feds dress up in carpet cleaning uniforms? She must be in bad trouble. Maybe she hasn't paid her taxes. Do they send the FBI after you for tax evasion? He wasn't sure.

"I haven't seen her in almost a month. I don't live in the area. I only come around and check my property every so often. Is she okay? Where is she?"

Fowler closed the apartment door behind him and said, "This is an ongoing investigation and we can't discuss it right now. Please give me your address and telephone number where you can be reached and someone will contact you soon. It is of the strictest importance that you say nothing to anyone about this. If so, Mr. Schmidt you can be charged with obstruction. Do I make myself clear?"

Schmidt nodded and did as the agent told him. He gave them his contact information and as he was leaving he overheard someone speaking low near the building.

"If we don't find Darcy Scott's kidnappers soon it may be too late for her."

Kidnapped! Darcy had been kidnapped. How horrible. Why hadn't he heard it on the news or the radio? The authorities should notify the press so that everyone can be looking for her. He always liked Darcy and now actually felt guilty thinking she was evading her taxes. If the police weren't going to help Darcy he would. With that thought, Arthur Schmidt placed a call to Channel 6 news. He knew the officer said he could be arrested for obstruction but weren't there rights like freedom of the press? He didn't have to give his name. He could just drop an anonymous tip so that everyone could be on the lookout for her. Yes, this was the right thing to do. Arthur was sure of it.

Chapter 33

The story broke on the evening news while Jonah and Katie were at a downtown bar trying to score a hit. Katie punched him in the arm and pointed to the TV over the bar. Darcy's picture was showing and the anchorman was talking.

"Bob! Turn that TV up!" Jonah screamed.

"The unknown source confirms that the FBI is currently investigating this unfortunate situation but the whereabouts of Miss Scott are still unknown. We will update you as any new information comes in."

"Holy shit," Katie whispered. "Jonah, what are we going to do? I thought you told her to tell them we would kill her if they called the police."

"I did," he hissed. "Don't panic. They'll never think to look for us. I'm sure they think she's been taken by some stranger with no ties to her. Some crazed fan, like that movie *Misery*. We'll never even cross their minds. We just need to lay low. I got somebody watching over this situation for me. We'll get our stuff and go home. Let's go."

Jonah finished his transaction with the man on the other side of the booth from them and left the bar.

Chapter 34

Davis was working late at his office. Most nights were spent pouring over transcripts but this night was doomed to be different. He had worked so often lately that he was even doing the work that his secretary usually did. It helped to keep busy. Ever since he heard that man talking to his mother last week he had been running from any confrontation with Kim. It was more than he could process. Jonah, the little brother that had always been there wasn't really his flesh and blood. Darcy came from the same parents as Jonah. Now he understood the overpowering love his parents had for Darcy while she lived with them. No doubt they saw the baby boy in her eyes and loved her even more because she was part of Jonah. Life had become more complicated than he could've ever have expected it to be. How do you accept that the parents whom you trusted more than anything lied to you?

He was putting away a file when his cell phone rang. Sliding it open he saw 'MOM' pop up on the display screen. Well, here was the conversation he had been trying to avoid for days.

"Hi Mom, what's up?"

"Hi honey, I just had a really strange phone call from a man named Michael. He said he used to be engaged to Darcy and it was urgent that he speak to you. He left his number for you to call him. He sounded very upset. Maybe you should call him back."

Davis didn't know what to say. Was this Michael the one who showed up ring in hand at her hotel that night? If so, 'what could he possibly want with me,' Davis thought.

"Ok Mom, give me the number and I'll give him a call."

"Davis, is there something wrong son? You have

hardly had two minutes for me in almost a week and don't think I haven't noticed that you've slept in town most nights."

"No Ma. There's nothing wrong. I've just been really busy at work. We can talk more about it later."

"You know I love you son, don't you?"

"Yes, Ma I know you love me and I love you but I just can't talk with you about things right now."

It seemed as if Kim knew that Davis needed more time. She would have to eventually tell him the truth but she just didn't know how right now. She at least needed to wait until she could find Jonah and talk to him first. She owed him that much. Davis would have to wait for now. She had no idea that Davis already knew and was putting off that same truthful conversation with her as well.

He copied down Michael's number and told his mother he would let her know if there was a problem. It felt like every time he almost got that woman out of his mind something happened to make him think of her. He wondered what it was this time. At the rate his family was going, it felt like every phone call was about to unlock a new secret.

Davis dialed the number Kim had given him to call Michael. He answered almost immediately.

"Hello? Is this Davis Boyden? We've met but not been introduced. My name is Michael Marshall. Darcy Scott and I used to see one another. Well, I'm sure you know that. Anyway, I'm calling because the story was on the news tonight and I didn't know who else to call. Darcy has been kidnapped and she's missing."

"Kidnapped? Oh my God! I don't want this to sound belligerent but first of all why would you think to call me? Second of all, what can I do?" Davis asked.

"Like I said, I didn't know who to call. I didn't know if you and Darce were still together or not. I haven't talked with her since our episode in Oklahoma. She doesn't have any family and I feel helpless. What happened with us was bad but I will always love her. I just thought maybe if I had someone who wanted to help we could assist the police in finding her. The time for hard feelings is over. Darce needs help."

Michael sounded almost as pitiful as Davis felt. The thought of someone hurting or mistreating Darcy was more than he could bear. This man went through a lot to find and contact him; he must really care about her. If Michael could put the past behind him, Davis was willing to do the same. After a short conversation, Davis made plans to fly out that night to New York. Michael agreed to meet him at the airport.

Davis called a good buddy of his who was also a lawyer and asked him to take over some of his immediate cases until he could get back. He went home, explained everything to his mother, packed a bag, and headed to the airport. Kim got down on her knees as her son's taillights disappeared into the distance and asked God to keep Darcy safe and to lead these men to her rescue. God had heard many prayers from Kim Boyden over the years but none as heartfelt as the last few months. So many needs that only He could handle.

"Dear Lord, please keep my children safe. Protect Jonah wherever he may be. Deliver Davis safely to New York. Keep Darcy from harm and help them all return home. Amen."

Chapter 35

Darcy was still lying on the futon when her two captors returned. She had tried to shift on her side where it wouldn't be so painful with her arms and legs bound. Her bladder was full and her mouth was dry. The blood from the cut on her head had dried in a big clump causing her hair to be stuck to the side of her face.

Jonah slammed the door with enough force to knock a cup off the kitchen counter. Darcy shuddered. He stomped into the front room and pointed an accusatory finger at Darcy.

"Your damn friend called the police. I've got a good mind to kill you right now."

She whimpered. 'Oh no Karen, what have you done?' she thought.

Jonah reached out and ripped the tape off of her mouth lightning fast. It felt like fire spread across her mouth. Darcy groaned.

"Please, Jonah. I need to go to the bathroom. Untie me please." He stared at her with a faraway look in his eyes.

"Jonah, are you hearing me? Please just let me go to the bathroom."

The drugs were kicking in and suddenly he didn't seem so mad at her or her friend but he still needed the money. Drugs cost money and he wasn't risking losing all that cash that someone would pay for a famous author by going all soft and fuzzy. He was also struggling to remember what else he was mad at her for. Family; it was something about family.

"I untie your feet and escort you myself to the bathroom. That's how it works. When we get back here you're going to make the ransom demands but be quick because I'm sure the cops are tracing the call. If you try to get away when I untie your feet, I will kill you and leave you to rot in this place. Do you understand me?"

His fingers were feeling numb and warm. He flexed them involuntarily.

"Yes, yes, anything just please don't hurt me."

Darcy was eager to say anything right now that would allow her to relieve the terrible stabbing pain in her kidneys and bladder. She didn't know how much longer she could hold it in.

He took her to the tiny little bathroom. It had lime green wallpaper with what must have been lilies on it long ago. It was so faded and dirty that all you could see were smudges of yellow on a stem. It didn't matter to her that she was being watched once she was able to use the restroom. She got to experience a moment of heaven. It felt so good to be able to relieve herself but best of all she got to walk with her feet untied. The circulation coming back into them felt like needles over her entire foot.

Jonah helped her to pull up her underclothes and her pants. He motioned for her to walk out of the bathroom in front of him.

When they returned to the front room he once again dialed the number of her friend Karen. He had two numbers written on a paper for her to read.

Karen answered the phone after the first ring. Agents jumped into action starting the recording machine and tracer.

"Karen, get a pen. Routing number is 0066185. Account number is 5648256. One million dollars by Friday at one p.m."

Jonah hit the cancel button on the phone and proceeded to remove the battery. A tear ran down Darcy's face. She knew it hadn't been long enough to trace. The GPS couldn't even be tracked with the battery removed.

"The call wasn't long enough. We couldn't trace. Did you hear anything that might let you know where she is? Did you hear anyone in the back ground?"

Karen couldn't recall anything to help. She felt so helpless. If there was anything at all that she could do but wait, it would make her feel better. This was awful. The agents were panicking because someone had leaked the story to the media. It was all over every channel. They were afraid that the exposure would have already sealed Darcy's fate. Karen had regretted calling the police because she was sure the kidnappers had already made good on their threat. All of them were relieved when the second ransom demand came in. It proved that they had not killed her. The FBI was working really hard to find out who had leaked the story but the problem at hand was how the news media had compromised their ability to find Darcy. The kidnappers would surely be more cautious now.

Darcy had hope for a brief moment that she would be able to keep the phone on long enough for a trace but Jonah made sure that didn't happen. Her hands were bound so she had no control over how long the conversation lasted. Jonah had all the control and he knew it. She still couldn't understand what she had done to deserve this. Where was Michelle? Where were Davis and the rest of the family? She prayed that someone somewhere would think to look for her in this rat hole before it was too late.

Davis arrived at the airport to find Michael waiting for him. The two men shook hands and gathered up the baggage. Michael took Davis to his house which was a nice Tudor style home in the Flagstone District. It was a lovely home that looked as if all it needed to come to life was a wife, a few kids, and a dog. Davis wondered if it were his fault that this man was lacking those things.

Michael lived in the beautiful home by himself. He still had not gotten over Darcy. He purchased the house a few days before he hopped a plane to surprise his beloved and surprise her he did! It was much more of a surprise for him than her. The contracts had already been signed so the bank had no sympathy on a man who lost his fiancé. The house was his. He moved in the next week but moving on was a whole other story. He was stuck in the past. Every empty room just reminded him of what could have been. She had called him several times after the initial incident but he just couldn't bring himself to allow her to see his hurt. He had turned inward with his pain; now it appeared that was all he had left.

Michael explained to Davis how going to the police for information would be useless. Neither one of them was blood related to Darcy and the police would not divulge information about an ongoing case to anyone who was not immediate family. Their only course of action was to drive around town and talk to anyone they could find. They could take photos to every street corner, every deli, and every supermarket. If they hit the street surely they were bound to find someone who knew something.

Chapter 36

Darcy awoke the next morning on the futon with her wrists burning. The tape was starting to bite into her arms. She could hear the sound of a radio coming from behind her in the kitchen. Pots and pans were banging. Katie came into the front room.

"I see you're awake. You hungry? I'm fixing food."

Darcy nodded. Her throat was so dry and her head pounded. She couldn't remember the last thing she had eaten. It seemed like a lifetime ago.

Katie went into the kitchen and came back with a plate that had eggs and toast on it. She sat it down on an old metal TV tray and grabbed Darcy's shoulder. Katie hauled her up into a sitting position. The sudden movements made her muscles scream out in agony.

"It isn't much but it will keep you from starving to death until you leave."

She looked down at Darcy's taped up hands.

"I don't guess you can eat like that can you? I'm going to get the gun. I'll untie your hands while you eat but if you try anything, I mean anything, I will shoot you. You're my ticket out of this dump. I thought Jonah was stupid for snatching you but he promised to take me away from this crap with all the money we're going to get, so I got to keep my eye on you honey."

Katie walked across the room and reached high to pull the gun off the shelf on a far wall and picked up a kitchen knife. She stuck the knife in the space between Darcy's wrists and the tape. The tape snapped free as she pulled the knife out.

Darcy immediately began to rub her wrists to stop the burning. It felt so good to be able to move them around. She was thirsting to death it seemed. The glass of water Katie had brought her was almost gone. She couldn't stop drinking. Finally she sat her glass down and started to eat her food. Darcy wanted to strike up a conversation but she wasn't sure where to begin.

"If you don't mind me asking, what's an attractive girl like you doing here in such a horrible neighborhood?"

Katie looked up quickly. Darcy knew Katie was not very attractive anymore but she had seen her before and knew she must have a very high opinion of herself. Her assumption was correct.

"Wrong place, wrong time honey. It works like that sometimes."

Darcy took another bite of eggs. "So, do you love him?"

Katie's eyes squinted. The look she gave Darcy was a mixture of humor and surprise. "Who, Jonah? Hell no. I wonder if I even like him sometimes but he serves his purpose. I'm hoping I can let him take me out of this place when they pay us for you. When I get to where we're going, he's history. I'm getting on with my life and he's not in the picture." Katie shrugged as if anyone with two eyes could see her point.

Darcy knew that now was not the time to try to push the subject. She needed more time alone to win Katie's trust, if that was even possible. The idea that Katie would trust anyone was foreign but one thing was for sure. It was whoever had the most cash and she believed she could convince her that Jonah needed to be cut out altogether. She just had to find the right way to make her believe it was her own idea. Darcy would have to tread lightly.

She finished breakfast with the gun still pointed in her direction. When the plate was removed she heard the door knob rattle.

Jonah was home.

She wasn't sure where he had been but he was still wearing the same clothes he had abducted her in. Bathing didn't seem to be high on anyone's list around here.

"What is she doing untied? Are you crazy? What if she got past you?"

Jonah was pacing the floor between the two rooms.

"I held her at gun point the whole time. How did you expect her to eat you dumbass!"

It was obvious that Katie was not accustomed to her judgment being challenged.

He shook his head violently. "Sometimes woman, you really are as dumb as you look."

Katie regarded him with as much concern as she would a mosquito. It infuriated him. She was not a woman to be trifled with. That was all the confirmation that Darcy needed to know who wore the pants in this operation. Now she could start planning what needed to be done.

Chapter 37

By the end of the next day Davis and Michael had drove all around the city talking to every man or woman on every street corner. They were coming up with nothing.

"Man, I need to stop somewhere and pick up a bite to eat. We've been at it all day and I'm starving," Davis complained.

"You sure you want to stop in this part of town? It looks pretty rough around here," Michael said.

Davis looked around at the rundown buildings and decided that it wouldn't be that bad to just stop into a local bar. It was better than rolling the dice by standing on the street corner, eating a vendor hot dog and getting jacked by a local thug.

They pulled up in front of a place call Smokey's Bar. It was a dark little hole in the wall with a few tables in the back and a couple of billiards tables. The guys grabbed a bar stool each and asked for a menu. The dark red wall paper made it look like a corner room in hell itself.

"Ordering food from this place may be a bad idea but damn if I'm not hungry enough to eat just about anything right now," Davis grumbled. The menu didn't offer a lot of choices.

They discussed what foods might be safe enough to try and mulled over their progress for the day, or lack of progress. Davis was sipping his beer when he noticed a man out of the corner of his eye. The man was wearing an old army jacket and had a shaggy beard but upon closer inspection it wasn't the man with the beard who caught his eye. It was the man he was talking to. The second man had his back turned to Davis. He was wearing a baseball cap with jeans and a tee- shirt. Something about the way he held himself reminded him of someone.

The bartender sat an order of hot wings on the bar and drew his attention away from the two men.

"What's wrong? Do you know those guys," Michael asked.

"No, I don't think so. I just thought for a minute that one of them looked familiar. I am an attorney so it's always possible that I've defended someone like him," Davis replied.

The hot wings were gone and they had drunk the last of their beer. It was time to go. Davis turned to pull out his wallet when he noticed the second man stand up to leave. The man turned and headed for the door completely oblivious to everyone else in the bar.

It was then that Davis realized that this man was a dead ringer for his brother Jonah. The only thing disturbing was this man looked really strung out. Jonah was always around 195 pounds and clean cut. This man looked like he couldn't be more than 130 pounds. His hair was falling in his eyes like he hadn't washed it in many weeks. His clothes were nasty and rumpled. Davis was frozen as the man left the bar.

"Sir, you going to pay me or what," the bartender asked rudely.

"Oh, sorry. I just thought I recognized that man. Do you know who he is?"

"Of course I know. I know every low life that comes in this place. His name's Jonah. Been coming here about five or six months now. I won't serve him anymore cause he owes me too much money. I cut out his tab. The only reason him and his woman come here's to see old John over there. He's probably the only dealer they don't owe money to." The bartender laughed at his own insight.

Davis couldn't respond right away. How in the hell did Jonah wind up here in New York? Had it really become bad enough to do drugs? Who is this woman the bartender talked about?

"Excuse me sir, do you know the woman's name that

118

he comes in with?" Davis was pulling out money from his wallet to pay the bill as he asked.

Bob talked while wiping off the glasses. "She's a rough looking sort. Looks like she's been around the block a while. I think her name's Cathy. Wait, no, it's Katie or Kate, I think."

Davis felt nauseated. His head began to swim violently. So they were here together. Of all the states and cities in the world, how did they end up here? Dear God, what if Jonah is here to harm Darcy. If he's sank so low to be on drugs he might even be so distorted as to act on the crazy ideas in his head about Darcy being his sister. Michael was staring at him with a confused look on his face, as if wondering who this man and his girlfriend were. He also thought he may have to pick his new found friend up off the floor at any minute.

Davis realized that he had to explain his behavior to Michael.

"That man is my brother and his lady friend, if you could call her that, is my ex-wife. I can't imagine what they would be doing here but I've got a bad feeling. You need to know the whole story. I'll tell you on the way out. Let's go."

Davis grabbed his coat. Michael was almost running to keep up with him.

"Where are we going?"

"We're going to see if we can find my brother. Something isn't right here and I want to know what it is. I'm just praying it isn't what I think it is."

The next morning Darcy woke up sore and stiff again. Jonah had left out early that morning, going God knows where. She knew he left because she heard him cough as he went out slamming the door. She was beginning to wonder if he ever slept. It must be the drugs. No human being could go that long without sleep and be normal. It took a while for Katie to get up and stirring. Darcy couldn't wait any longer.

"Katie can I please use the bathroom?"

She looked up, surprised, as if she forgot for a moment that Darcy was taped up on her futon.

"Sure. Guess you're probably wishing you had a bath huh? It's been a few days."

Darcy actually felt a bit of excitement at the idea.

"I would love a bath but if Jonah came in and seen that you let me shower you would be in a lot of trouble and I don't want to see him get angry with you."

Katie's head snapped back as if she heard something she couldn't believe. She pointed her finger at Darcy as she said, "Jonah Boyden doesn't tell me what I can and can't do. If I wanna let you take a bath then By God that's exactly what I'll do. I'm through letting men take advantage of me. It's time that I called the shots my way!"

Katie looked quite pleased with herself for making the declaration. It was as if the subject was closed and her word was final.

Darcy was so pleased that she got the response she was looking for, that she almost smiled. Katie would cut off her nose to spite her face if it made her point. That was obvious. Good. That's just what she had been hoping for the whole time.

"Get up. I got some clothes you can fit into. You're going to get a shower."

Darcy was so excited about the thought of showering after several days that she was tempted to cry. Katie hauled her up and made her hop to the bathroom. Once inside Katie pulled the gun off the shelf and told Darcy plainly, "I'm going to untie your hands, not your feet. I'll be right outside this door and if you try to come out or get away, I will shoot you. Do you understand?"

Darcy nodded hoping she would just hurry up and let her take the first shower she had in days. Katie cut the tape on her wrists and helped her into the tub. She walked out and closed the door behind her.

Darcy tried to experiment with her new found partial freedom. It helped to have her hands loose but her legs had been bound for so long the tape had melted together like glue. She was going to have to rip her pants to get them off. She knew that her new friend with the gun would be back any second to check on her. Luckily her lounge pants she had been wearing when she was taken were thin and easy to tear off her body even with her legs taped. All she could do was try to bathe and think of her next move.

Katie was back within minutes. She opened the door and threw an old cotton nightgown on the sink. It was something Darcy could wear without having to untie her feet. This girl was sharper than she gave her credit for.

Jonah didn't return until late evening and he was so absorbed with sitting at the kitchen table and getting high that he never noticed she was wearing different clothes.

Around nine o'clock he shuffled into the front room and turned on the television. That was when he noticed Darcy's appearance.

"Why are you in different clothes? Your hair looks damp. Katie! Why is she dressed in your stuff and why does she look bathed? What the hell did you do?"

"She needed a bath. She was starting to smell so I let her bathe. What's it to you?"

Jonah jumped to his feet. He strode across the room with such force that you could feel the floor shake. In the blink of an eye he swung the back of his hand at Katie and connected with her face. She fell back across the kitchen floor. He jumped on top of her and started screaming as he was shaking her up and down. She flopped around like a rag doll beneath Jonah.

"You stupid tramp! You think cause you led every other man around by the crotch that you can do it to me? You're wrong. I buy your dope and keep your sorry ass alive and for what? You aren't even any good to me in bed anymore. You're lucky I don't kill you right now! Get up! I'm going out and when I get back you better be gone!"

He got up off of Katie and stormed out the door. Katie sat on the floor for what seemed like twenty minutes crying and shivering. Darcy was watching her only hope going out the window quick. Panic was rising up. She had to do something fast. If she let Katie leave she would never get away and something inside of her told her that this was more than a regular kidnapping for cash. Her intuition said that if she didn't escape she wouldn't make it out alive.

"Katie are you okay? I'm so sorry he did this. You deserve better. If you let me go, you and I can get out of here. I'll give you enough money to make it on your own. I'll help you get a job if you want to go back to doing hair. You don't need him. I can help you if you help me."

Katie cut her eyes at Darcy as she was adjusting her clothes. "You must be dumber than you think I am. As soon as I let you go, you call the cops. That's a fact. I know that and you know that. You don't even know me or like me. I'm a washed up beautician with a drug addiction that even you can't afford. If you hadn't come along none of us would be here so thanks but no thanks. I'm leaving."

Darcy began to cry. She knew that there was no amount of talking that would make Katie free her. What would it be like here without her? She was the only one who had shown her any compassion or care. Jonah would make Darcy pay for this also, she was sure of it.

Katie emerged from the bedroom about fifteen minutes later with two satchel bags. She had one thrown over each shoulder. It looked like she was going to leave without any further conversation until she stopped midway out the door.

"You know, I don't know what happened with you and

Davis but whatever it was, he really cared for you. I saw it in his eyes. Take that for what it's worth."

She never looked back as she walked out and closed the door.

Darcy spent the next hour crying. She cried for the situation she was in. She cried for Michael, for Davis, for her real mother, and for everything she believed she would miss when she died in this rat hole. The only thing to do now was to pray.

Chapter 38

The guys had rode around for hours that night but still couldn't catch up with Jonah. It was as if he had just walked out into the night and disappeared. Davis wasn't prepared to give up though. He had shared all the information he had with Michael. He told him what the man told his mother about Darcy being Jonah's sister. It explained why he had such a bad feeling about the whole situation. Jonah was a loose cannon and there was no telling what he would do if he did have Darcy. The police couldn't know about this. Davis knew he had to find them himself. There would be no other way to get to the bottom of it all.

The next night he and Michael were sitting across the street from the same bar hoping to catch a glimpse of Jonah again. Michael wasn't sure if he agreed with Davis' theory but right now this was all they had to go on and if there was a chance of finding Darcy, he would go along with it. Any lead was a good lead.

Boredom was beginning to set in. Four hours of staring across the road at all manner of drunks passing in and out of Smokey's Bar was starting to feel hopeless when Davis noticed a guy coming down the street with a hooded jacket pulled up over his head. He noticed the gait immediately.

"Look, there he is."

Michael sat up quickly.

"Are we going in after him or just wait to see what he does?"

Davis nodded his head slowly.

"No, we're going to wait on him and follow him."

It took about ten minutes for Jonah to come back out of the bar. He walked out and turned to the right. They pulled out slowly and followed him from a distance. He was walking quickly with his hands in his jacket and his head down. The old gray jacket didn't appear to be keeping the cold off of him judging by how deeply he had his hands buried in the pockets. He made it about a block and a half when he ducked into an old apartment building. The paint on the front doors was a dark color that was almost peeled completely off. They pulled the car over to the side of the street.

"You think this is where he lives?" Michael asked. "You think Darcy might be here?"

"I'm not sure. We'll wait a minute and if he doesn't come out, I'm going in. You can wait here if you want."

"No, we're in this together. If you go in, I go in."

Jonah came blasting in the door of the little apartment like he always did. He stopped short when he saw Darcy.

"You've been crying. Why? What you got to cry about? Is the whore gone? She better be."

He fired questions at her but didn't give her time to answer any of them. He stalked into the bedroom, probably searching to see if Katie was really gone. Darcy was scared to even speak to him. She decided silence was her best chance at avoiding whatever crazy punishment he could inflict.

She could hear him in the other room talking to someone. He couldn't be on the telephone because she was looking at the phone in front of her. He had to be talking to himself. Fear was beginning to become overwhelming in her mind. Jonah was in some type of drug induced psychotic episode. She could hear him talking about getting rid of a sister. He doesn't have a sister. He was losing touch with reality. It was now or never, she had to get away.

Darcy's only way out was the front door or the fire escape but she knew she would never make it to the front door in time and if she did she didn't have the key to unlock the internal lock on it. Jonah had obviously changed the lock to a special type you had to have a key to open when he hatched the idea to kidnap her. When left alone earlier she also saw that the fire escape was broken and it was a long fall down. Now was the time to decide the lesser of two evils, Jonah or a broken limb.

Suddenly the sound of the closet being slammed in the bedroom propelled her into motion. Darcy pushed her weight off the futon and managed to get into a standing position. She would be forced to literally hop to the window. It was difficult to hop quietly and it was a slow pace. It took several minutes to make it across the room. The last thing she wanted to do was have him hear the bumping of her moving around and bring him in to check on her.

Once she reached the window, she braced herself carefully so she would be able to use both hands to pull up the window pane. She was almost home free as long as she didn't break her neck on the jump. It seemed that she could feel every nerve ending. Her pulse was racing at top speed. "Life or death Darcy, life or death," she told herself. Over and over in her head she had to keep assuring herself that she could do this. She quietly offered up a prayer for her very life and began to hoist herself onto the window sill.

"I'm tired of waiting. I'm going in," Davis barked.

Michael jumped up to adjust his coat. "I'm with you, let's go."

The guys jumped out of the car and made their way across the deserted street and up to the front door of the dilapidated building. Michael turned the knob and the door squeaked open. Years of rust and dirt screamed out in protest. Once inside, they weren't sure where to go. It appeared that there were several apartment doors and none of them were named. They could faintly hear the sounds of living going on; kids crying, TV sets blaring, and even a dog barking. Davis couldn't believe that his big time brother wound up living in such poverty. How could this have happened?

Darcy flipped her body out the window. Her hands were still taped and she couldn't support her full weight so, before she knew it, she slipped. It happened so quickly that she couldn't scream or stop it. She fell and God answered her prayer. Someone had placed a large refrigerator box alongside of the building full of some type of plastic. Darcy hit the box. The pain in her side shot through her like a hot knife. The box slowed her down and saved her life but it didn't keep her from the hard thud she made on the pavement below. The tape still bit into her ankles and it caused her to roll in a side motion that made her sure she had damaged her hip. The pain was radiating in waves down her leg.

The thought came to her immediately that Jonah would miss her any minute and come looking. She had to move past the pain and hide. This was her life she was fighting for; there was no time for pain now. The piercing feeling in her chest was getting worse; it was causing her to be unable to take a full breath. She noticed an old dumpster at the end of the alley. It was pushed up against a building.

Darcy drug herself up the alley realizing that every minute that passed might be her last. When she reached the end she saw the small opening behind the dumpster. It was vitally important for her to fit her body into that opening. It was the only way she could be hidden. If she went out into the street bound and tied she would never make it to freedom. In this neighborhood it would be more likely that she would be raped and beaten by someone on the street.

After what seemed like an hour but was only seconds, she managed to wedge her body into the tight confinement. She couldn't see out but that was alright because that meant no one could see in either. It was safety, at least for now.

Davis and Michael were walking into the dimly lit hallway when a man exited one of the apartments. He stopped short when he saw the men. Davis spoke first.

"Do you know where Jonah Boyden lives in here?"

The man's eyebrows shot up. "You mean that whack job? Sure. He lives upstairs in 4C. You police or hit men?"

The man must have found his comment funny because he laughed heartily. Davis nodded his thanks and bounded up the stairs two at a time with Michael right behind him.

Chapter 39

Jonah was at his breaking point. Nothing was going right. Katie had betrayed him and left him just like his ex-wife. His drug addled mind was forgetting that he forced her to leave him after he slapped her around on the kitchen floor. He was probably going to get beat out of his money he was expecting if he got the pay off on Darcy. This whole situation was starting to seem like he was the one getting the short end of the stick. He was the bad guy as always. No wonder his mom and dad treated Davis better. He was their real son, not an imposter like Jonah. That's why Jonah was such a bad kid and constantly got punished for doing wrong. It was in his blood. The same blood that ran through Darcy's veins.

She was his sister the whole time. That's why his mom and dad wanted so badly to keep her when she came to live with them. They liked her more than Jonah. She was just another kid to take his place, he thought. They probably wished it had been Darcy that his real parents gave them instead of him.

Jonah's mind was unraveling with all these wild thoughts. His head was hurting. The pain just kept getting worse as the memories and thoughts ran through his brain.

When Michelle left and took the baby it didn't seem like a big deal. He used his misfortune as an excuse to grab Katie and move to New York. She always wanted to go to the big city and Jonah had plenty of money to oblige her. It was a nonstop party. They stayed at the best hotels, ate at the best restaurants, hung out with the coolest people, and did the premium drugs. It wasn't long before the money was dwindling down. Jonah had left his job under bad feelings with the company. Katie had no job in the city and both of them had a drug problem that just wouldn't take a day off. The downward spiral happened so fast that before they knew it, they were living in a dump and owing every low life bookie and drug dealer more money than they could scrounge up.

Jonah made a trip back home to pack up the house he had shared with Michelle so he could sell everything in it before the bank took it away. It was a needed trip anyway. He could certainly use the money he would get from selling off all the furniture and appliances. It would be a financial infusion to keep him and Katie going a while longer.

He ran into town to pick up some things from a local store when he noticed a man watching him from across the street. That man would change his pathetic life forever. That man would show him the truth about his life that he could've never imagined. Part of him wished that man would have never looked in his direction. Never told him about Darcy.

He had fumed over the truth that his real father had told him for over a week when he received the call from a blocked number. The man wouldn't give him a name but he did tell Jonah that he was willing to pay a lot of money for someone to do a job for him. The strange man on the phone knew his secret. He knew that Darcy was his sister and he convinced Jonah that he could get rid of the bitch AND make a whole lot of money at the same time.

Jonah thought his life was finally looking up when he began this plan but now he wasn't so sure about anything.

Jonah was frustrated. He needed a drink. "I wonder if she even left me beer."

He opened the door of the bedroom to make his way into the kitchen when he felt a draft. Suddenly he realized the window was open and the room was empty. Darcy was gone.

His mind went blank.

Jonah rushed to the window and looked out.

"Damn it! How could she jump tied up? Where the

hell is she?"

It was at that moment, the knocking on the door started. It was probably Katie begging to come home. He didn't have time for her drama right now. He had real problems. Of course, she was probably the one to blame for this mess. Katie probably helped Darcy escape. He was going to teach them both a lesson this time. Forget the money; he would rather kill them both right now! Jonah bolted to the door and jerked it open, ready to swing his fist at the woman he thought was knocking.

It wasn't Katie; it was Davis and another man.

"How did you find me and what do you want?" Jonah kept scratching his nose nervously and looking behind his guests into the hallway.

Could this possibly get any worse? His hostage had escaped, his brother had found him, and if he didn't get a handle on things, he could be going to prison really soon.

"I want to come in. Is that okay with you? I am still your brother aren't I?"

The thought of playing the 'brother card' with him disgusted Davis but he knew he had to get into that apartment. He had to see for himself if Darcy was there or had been there at all.

Jonah didn't know what to do. He couldn't let Davis and this man who might be the police in here because he had to find Darcy before she sent every cop in the world right to his front door. If he didn't let them in, it would appear that he had something to hide. He had no choice. He stepped aside to let the men enter.

Davis walked into the cramped space and glanced around. Michael seemed to be silently observing.

Jonah was as nervous as a chicken on a chopping block and Davis could sense it. His hands kept going in and out of his pants pockets like he didn't know where they belonged. The smell of mildew was thick in the air. Katie didn't seem to be here and if she was, it was obvious that her cleaning skills had not improved since they had been married. The place was filthy.

"So, to what do I owe this honor," Jonah remarked sarcastically. Davis had to think quickly so that he could continue to look for any clues that might lead them to Darcy.

"I was in town for business and I thought I saw you in a bar one night. When I realized it was you, I asked around and found out where you lived. I wanted to see how you were doing and see what brings you to the city."

"Don't act like we're friends brother. I know you don't like me and that's no love loss. I had some friends up here and I thought I would visit. I had some cash flow problems and decided to stay. Now, if that's all you want to know, you and your friend can leave the way you came in."

"This is a business acquaintance of mine named John, just so you know. So where's Katie? I hear you two have made a lasting bond."

Davis was still continually scanning the small room. It was cold in the apartment. Wonder why he has that blasted window up in the middle of winter, Davis thought.

"Katie left. I grew tired of her so if you don't mind, could you go? I have an appointment I have to get to."

For some reason Davis kept staring at the open window. It looked so out of the ordinary that it was bothering him.

"Sure brother. We'll go but you better close this window before you catch pneumonia."

Davis made his way to the window and started to pull it closed when he noticed a single long dark hair on the sill. He looked down at the distance from the window to the street. The ladder was broken. If she had been here and left through this window she would surely have fallen to her death.

Davis motioned for Michael to follow him out. Jonah was right on their heels practically pushing them out the door. Davis turned to say goodbye to his brother and

Jonah closed the door in his face.

"So, what do you think?" Michael asked.

Davis held up the hair for him to see.

"I think this isn't my ex-wife's hair and it sure looks a lot like Darcy's."

"There are millions of women in this country with hair like that. How can you be so sure it's hers?"

"I know it is. Why would someone have the window open in winter? Why would this hair be on the window sill to start with? I think we are closer to finding her than we think. I have a strong instinct that never leads me wrong. Something is up and I'm sure it involves Darcy."

Davis ran down the stairs and into the street. If she went out the window it was a desperate act. She had to be close. He could feel her.

"Hey Mike, I'm going down the street and look around. Maybe she tried to go to a neighbor for help. You go into that alley and see what you can find."

Michael pulled the hood up on his jacket and ducked his head against the wind. He darted into the alley and looked around. He moved boxes and bags of trash but he found nothing.

Darcy heard someone moving around. She didn't make a sound in case it was Jonah looking for her. She had only been outside for about thirty minutes but the cold was beginning to creep into her bones. She had no coat, no blanket, nothing more to cover her than the old night gown Katie had given her to wear. She would freeze to death before long if she didn't think of some way to get out unseen and get help. The sound of footsteps was getting closer. She was praying that it wouldn't end this way.

Someone was talking. She could hear them over the sound of the wind whipping through the alley. It wasn't Jonah, of that she was sure but she couldn't make out what they were saying. It was definitely a man. He must be on the telephone because she could hear the formation of a one way conversation.

"What do you mean, she's just GONE? No one is just gone! She had to get out some way. I want her found immediately and the ransom will take place first thing in the morning. If they don't want to play ball then you have my permission to kill her and I will personally pay you the money owed to you. This is becoming a thorn in my side. You bungled this thing up from the beginning. Now, do as I say and I will call back at seven tomorrow morning. Do not let me down."

Darcy wasn't sure at first, but now she knew who she was hearing just on the other side of the dumpster.

It was Michael.

She risked sliding to the right enough to see around the enclosure. He was standing there with his jacket closed tight talking on his cell phone. Her mind was reeling. Michael had arranged this horrible thing to happen to her and now she might still die because of a man that once loved her. He slid his phone shut and headed out of the alley.

Davis returned to the front of the building and soon after Michael reappeared from the alley. "Anything at all?" Davis asked.

"Nope. Not a thing. I think we're barking up the wrong tree man. Your brother's a strange character but he doesn't strike me as someone who's organized enough to execute a kidnapping. You also have to take into consideration that there's just no way she could've gone out that window and lived. We need to head back to the hotel and try again tomorrow."

Davis reluctantly agreed and climbed into the car. What Mike said made sense but the whole scenario here sure didn't. His intuition was nagging at him and he couldn't let go of the feeling that she was near. As they pulled out into the street they didn't know that the very thing they were looking for was right under their noses.

Jonah never bothered to look in the alley for his hostage. He was too busy screaming and punching the furniture. He had no idea how to find her and it wouldn't be long before the Feds were at his door or worse. The mystery man who hired him to do this job was badly pissed off. He had said so on the phone only minutes ago. No matter what he did, his ass was grass if he couldn't produce Darcy. The idea of personal revenge no longer mattered to him. He was more concerned with self-preservation. He had to get out of here and do it fast.

It only took ten minutes for Jonah to throw his few clothes in a bag, zip his coat up, and run out of the building. He didn't even bother to lock the door to the crummy little apartment. Who cares? He would never come back to it anyway.

Chapter 40

Darcy knew that her options were few. The choices were death from hypothermia or running for somewhere warm to get much needed medical help and safety.

She managed to drag herself from the crack behind the dumpster. Her ribs were burning from the pain and she could hardly walk. Her fingers had lost all feeling from the cold and it was hard to take in a breath.

It had taken many excruciating minutes to make it to the front of the alley when she heard the building entrance door slam. She leaned behind the gutter pipe that was on the adjacent building to hide in case it was Jonah. The cold was making her bare feet turn dark purple and it felt like knives sticking in the bottoms of her toes.

It was in fact Jonah coming out of the building but he didn't even look her way. He had a bag in his hand and he sprinted past her in a hurry. She was very confused about what was going on. She saw an opportunity that was dangerous but she felt she had no other choice. Darcy decided to go back to the apartment. She needed warm clothes. She knew she had to raise her body temperature or she would soon go into shock. From what she had seen, Jonah was leaving and it made her feel confident he wouldn't be back soon judging from the bag on his arm and the speed he was traveling. From the looks of the neighborhood there would be no safe haven of help. Her only real chance was to warm up, dress for the weather, and get to some type of normal civilization.

After making sure the coast was clear, she hobbled into the building and up the stairs. The pain was rapidly increasing. She had been unconscious when they brought her here but she knew the direction to go by determining where the window she jumped from was.

"Please God don't let the door be locked," she

whispered. The walk up the stairs was torture. She needed medical attention and she needed it fast. Once she was at the door she put her hand on the knob and the door swung open. Relief flooded her. Darcy never thought she would be so relieved to be entering this rat hole again.

She went immediately to the bedroom to look for warm clothes. All she could find was an old torn bathrobe that wasn't much better than what she had on but she donned it anyway. Suddenly she remembered seeing the phone sitting on a table in the living room.

She stumbled to the phone and picked it up but there was no dial tone. That must be why she never saw anyone use it. Cell phones were the only phones she actually witnessed anyone ever use.

Darcy crumpled on the floor and cried. She knew she wasn't in any shape to go back into the cold again. The cold had affected her body worse than she had thought at first. Her hip definitely wouldn't carry her back out again no matter how warm she got and she couldn't stay here in case he came back. It seemed like she had hit a brick wall. She was at the end of her rope.

Davis pulled into the parking area of the hotel. He ran his hands through his mane of dark hair.

"Mike, I'm going to take a drive and clear my head. I won't be gone long. You round us up some food and I'll see you soon."

"Sure man. You take a drive and relax. I'll see what I can find and when you get back we'll go over what we want to do tomorrow."

Davis had no intention of clearing his head. He had every intention of going back to that apartment and beating Jonah until he came clean. There were few times in his life that Davis had ignored his intuition and each time he had suffered for it. He would not make the same mistake again. He had come all this way to find this woman and he was not giving up so easily.

Chapter 41

Michael was glad his partner needed some alone time. That gave him the opportunity to go back to the building and snoop around. She surely left some clue as to how she got away. Maybe she was dragged down the alley and covered up by some sicko who wanted to come back and enjoy her later. Either way, he needed to find her. He was not going to let this plan fall apart now after all his efforts.

Darcy shouldn't have underestimated him. She always thought he was so clean cut. She thought she could just play him off the way she did and never suffer any consequences for it. What a joke! He might have gotten over it if she hadn't kept calling to apologize. How dare she? Did she really think she could screw someone else and just call to say 'I'm sorry?' He had too many months to think about how she destroyed him and when the opportunity presented itself to pay her back, he took it.

It was an act of fate to get a call from Marco Bennett that day. Mr. Bennett had tracked his long lost daughter down but couldn't get a number for her. Someone had tipped him off that Michael was her fiancé so Marco called him. Mr. Bennett had an amazing story to tell indeed. It was a story that Michael decided he could use to his advantage. The sick little family circle going on in Oklahoma would be the way he would get revenge for what that tramp did to him. Michael had been pushed to the breaking point and decided he would contact Jonah Boyden and goad him into his plan. It only made things easier when he realized that Jonah already knew about the dirty family secrets. It didn't take much effort to anonymously offer him large amounts of money to kidnap Darcy. He told him he could keep the ransom money plus the money he would pay him to do the job. The greedy bastard couldn't say no. It was a dream come true. All he had to do was walk him through how to kidnap her and how to demand the ransom. Once that part was over he promised Jonah he could kill Darcy any way he saw fit. Not once did Jonah ever ask Michael's name. He was totally nameless and faceless in the situation. That was good for him in case it all blew up.

The yellow cab let Michael out in front of the building. The cabbie was a true New Yorker, he took a lesser known short cut and Michael was back in ten minutes. Jonah didn't know that it was he who set him on this path but he was about to find out. He never intended on revealing his identity to that moron but if it meant getting things back on track he would just have to do it.

When Michael reached the apartment door he heard sobbing. It didn't sound like a man. He cracked open the door and to his amazement, Darcy was lying on the floor crying. She looked up suddenly and her face was panic stricken.

He didn't expect to find her nor did he expect for her to see him at all. He had to think on his toes.

"Oh my God! Darce! I found you. Are you OK?"

He ran towards her with arms outstretched attempting to play the concerned friend. She drew away from him and screamed.

"Get away from me! Don't come near me!"

Michael looked puzzled. Did she know? How could she know?

"Honey, please let me help you. The police and I have been searching for you for days. Darce, no one's going to hurt you again."

He was inching closer and she was cowering away from him. She had to know something.

"You liar! I know you did this. Stay away from me. You're crazy!" She seemed to be gasping for each breath she took.

Michael knew she was a smart woman and it didn't matter how she knew. All that mattered was that she did know and it was time to play or fold. He dropped his head and began to laugh.

"You thought I was just going to forgive you for shattering my future huh? You make me sick. I came to propose to you, give you a great life and a family. Something you never had. You told me so. How did you repay me? What did you give me? A kick in the ass, that's what! Now it's my turn to take my pound of flesh you bitch!"

Darcy was shivering. How could she have slept with someone that she never knew? This man in front of her was deeply disturbed. She knew there was no escape and she wasn't even going to try. The pain in her body had consumed her; she was weak and broken. It was over. She silently prayed that God would hold her life in his hands one last time.

Michael leaned over her and shook his head. He pulled a knife out of his jacket. The blade gleamed in the light. Darcy could feel the tears running down her face. She had moved past fear and into a place where there was no feeling, no being, just blackness. Shock covered up the reality of the blade slicing into her body. There was nothing for Darcy but quiet peace.

Chapter 42

Davis parked his car across the road from the run down building and ran dodging traffic to get to the other side of the street. He pulled open the door and leaped up the stairs. The feeling of urgency had gotten so strong that he felt like every minute would be the difference between life and death. When he reached the apartment he noticed the door was slightly ajar.

Instinct took over. Davis kicked the door open and saw Michael swinging a knife into Darcy's crumpled body on the floor. He dove on top of Michael and both men rolled to the opposite side of the room. The knife went skittering across the floor.

It took a moment for Davis to process what was going on but he never slowed down his fight for Darcy's life.

Michael was behind this the whole time. Michael, the man who claimed to have once loved her enough to make her his wife. The man who faked concern and went far enough to bring Davis miles away from home just to pretend to search for her.

It was all clear now.

He brought Davis here because he knew Darcy wouldn't be found alive and he wanted to punish him for taking her away from him. In his mind it was one big punishment. He just wasn't sure how he got Jonah involved in it all.

The idea that this man tricked him, drug Jonah into it, and above all, hurt Darcy, was too much to take. A rage that he had never known swelled up in Davis. He threw Michael away from him and in one fluid motion he picked up a large glass ashtray and crashed it into the side of Mike's skull. The man went down like the Titanic. Blood squirted from a gash in this head and leaked out onto the floor.

Davis scrambled over to Darcy. She was unconscious and bleeding badly. She barely had a pulse. Looking at her so helpless made him want to scream. He could admit now that he loved this woman and always had. If she died, he would never forgive himself for not realizing that sooner. He grabbed his cell phone and dialed 911. All he could do was hold pressure on the wound while he waited for help. He prayed hard as the sirens got closer and closer. He was still on his knees when the EMS workers and police arrived with a familiar man right on their heels.

Chapter 43

Darcy was beginning to awaken. She couldn't move very well and as she managed to pry open her eyes, she saw why. Bandages were all over her body and she had tubes running into parts that she couldn't completely feel.

"Sweetie, don't move. I'll get the doctors."

Davis? That was Davis. What happened? What was Davis doing here? Where was she?

Doctors and nurses came rushing into the room. A tall grey-headed man was the first to speak.

"Miss Scott, I'm Dr. Carson. You're in the University Medical Center. You've suffered a few stab wounds but thankfully no major organs were hit. You lost a lot of blood; you have a broken leg, and a few broken ribs. You have been asleep for three days. Do you remember anything that happened to you?"

At first it was fuzzy then Darcy suddenly saw the whole episode unfold. She cried while she tried to recount her ordeal to her doctor and to the detectives that were present. Davis held her hand the whole time. When she finished she looked at Davis and asked, "Why did you come for me?"

"Because I love you and your family loves you and you can't leave just yet. You have someone you have to meet."

That was when she noticed an older man standing in the doorway of her hospital room. He was someone she had never met before but he seemed strangely familiar.

"Darcy, this man's name is Marco Bennett. He's your father and if it weren't for him coming to the farm last week, we may not have found you in time."

She wasn't sure she heard Davis correctly when he said this man was her father but when he repeated himself, there was no denying it. She started to shake her head and object to his presence after all these years but Davis stopped her.

"Please Darcy. There is a story you need to hear. You need to finally know the truth after all these years."

She could see the sincerity in the eyes of both men so she gave in and motioned for the man to sit by her bed. Marco told her the story of her life in great detail. He was honest and caring and spared no explanation. She was shocked, amazed and more than a bit shaken but she was relieved to finally fill some of the missing holes in her life. So many things made sense now; she knew who she was and why.

The past was at last clear but the future was still really foggy. That was something that all of them would have to work on, one day at a time.

Chapter 44

Jonah Boyden was found the following day by beat police in an abandoned building just two blocks from where he held Darcy hostage. He had suffered a massive heart attack brought on by a heroin overdose. It seemed that he had died as lonely as he had lived.

Davis had the body flown back to Oklahoma for burial beside their father. Kim would have it no other way. He was her baby boy despite everything. She would always love him anyway. Michelle declined to be a part of the arrangements.

Michael Marshall was arrested for kidnapping, conspiracy to commit a crime, false imprisonment, attempted murder, and many other charges that would ensure he would never walk the streets as a free man again. His family severed all ties with him in shame and cut off any and all financial support. Darcy received a letter from the Marshall family expressing their deepest apologies and offering any help she could ever need in the future.

Darcy was released from the hospital after two weeks. Davis was with her day and night throughout her ordeal and was the one to drive her home to her apartment. He hired a crew to pack up her flat and ship her things to Oklahoma. Darcy returned with Davis to the ranch. She was still weak physically and emotionally but she knew she had the promise of a new beginning and that meant more to her than she could've hoped for.

The plane ride was exciting to Darcy because she knew that she was heading home to stay for the first time in many years. The doctors released her to travel back to Oklahoma so she could begin her new life. Davis and she would stay at the ranch until they could find a house somewhere close. She didn't want to be too far away from Kim and the rest of the family. Her family.

She knew she couldn't have asked for better. Davis had been at her side the whole time and throughout her recovery. It was clear that life had given them a second chance. They never discussed the future except for the fact that they would be together. No one wanted to rush things. There was still so much past to sort out and so many losses to grieve. There would be time for happiness later.

The plane landed and Davis helped her to his car in the parking garage at the airport. The drive home was the most beautiful sight she had ever seen. Strange how just knowing that you're driving toward your loved ones can make the whole world prettier, Darcy thought.

Davis suddenly pulled off the road that led out to the ranch and came to a stop. He turned to Darcy and pulled a handkerchief out of the glove compartment.

"I have a surprise for you so you have to wear this over your eyes until I say you can take it off. Is it a deal?"

"A surprise? Haven't we all had enough surprises in the last few weeks? Well, I guess I can suffer for the sake of getting a present," she giggled. Too much laughter made her ribs hurt. Some of the injuries still felt fresh because of the severe bruising.

He tied the handkerchief around her head snuggly and she felt the vehicle begin to move forward. Darcy felt like a little girl again, only this time she had something to be happy about.

The car drove through the gates and into the yard and stopped. Davis got out and came around to her door and opened it for her.

"Let me hold your arm. We can't have you falling out

of the car and hurting yourself your first day home."

Darcy was giddy. She couldn't imagine what gift he had for her. She could feel him leading her across the lawn. The grass was soft under her shoe. The cool wind felt fresh against her face.

He stopped short and reached for the tie to unfasten the blindfold. When it dropped from her eyes, the scene was not what she ever thought it would be. They were standing in front of the old rope bridge. The ropes were decorated with white ribbons and white roses. Red roses adorned the rails to the steps. A small pillow trimmed in lace sat on the middle of the bridge. Darcy couldn't catch her breath. Tears were streaming down her face.

Davis gently pulled her toward the steps that led up to the bridge. He motioned for her to go up. She made the few steps to the top with his hands guiding her. Once both of them were on top he walked out onto the bridge, knelt down, and retrieved a small box off the pillow. She watched him turn to kneel in front of her.

"Darcy Scott, I love you more than I have ever thought I could love someone. You are the best thing that ever happened to me. I want to make you my wife. I want us to have children and for our children to be able to stand here where we are now. I want to make you happy. Will you marry me?"

Davis opened the box and nestled inside black velvet was a single-stoned diamond engagement ring.

"I had so many to choose from but this ring stood out more than any other. I chose it because I wanted it to be like you. You Darcy, are my one perfect diamond. You and only you. So what do you say? Will you let me cherish you forever?"

Tears were streaming down her face and running into the collar of her shirt but she didn't even notice it.

"Oh Davis. I don't know what to say. You've said everything that I ever dreamed of hearing a man say to me. I wish I could sound as eloquent as you right now but

I'm speechless. All I can say is, YES. Yes, I will marry you!"

Chapter 45

The wedding plans began immediately. There was so much to do! Darcy's publicist and few friends would be flying in for the wedding. It was scheduled for the spring and it would be held at the ranch. She had even asked Marco to give her away. If Albert had been alive she would have been honored to have him stand in as her father but he would be watching from above on her special day. She had been spending time with Marco since she had arrived home and they were creating a nice relationship between them. He was trying really hard to make up for lost time and she was trying hard to give him the benefit of the doubt.

The holidays were fast approaching and the whole Boyden household was getting ready by decorating. Michelle had forged a friendship with Darcy. It was amazing to see the woman that was too scared to carry on a conversation when she was married bloom into the outgoing, smart, and sassy woman she was becoming. The two were inseparable. She especially loved to babysit A.J. He was a lovely child and very smart for his age. While Davis worked in town at his office, Michelle and Darcy would often take the baby for walks.

As he grew older she could see so much of his father in him, her brother. It was still hard for her to think of Jonah that way. She wished things could have been different. To grow up with a real brother would have been great. That couldn't be a reality so she chose to give that love to little A.J. She was a doting aunt and she couldn't wait until she could give A.J. a younger cousin to play with.

The idea of being a mother never really crossed her mind until now. She was intrigued by the thought of having her own little one that she and Davis could spoil. Oh how different her child's life would be compared to the one she had. Her baby would never know loneliness and indifference. He or she would be loved beyond measure with a big family. It was all she had ever dreamed of for a child of hers.

This particular day Michelle and Darcy were in the den with the baby when a car pulled into the driveway. Michelle looked out the large picture window and gasped. "Dear Lord. What does she want? How could she show up here after everything that happened?"

Darcy wasn't sure who Michelle could be talking about until she peeped out the other window and saw Katie walking up to the porch. Darcy had never told the police that Katie was involved with Jonah in her kidnapping. Davis wanted to tell them but she had forbid it. Something inside of her knew that Katie had already received her own punishment for what she had done in life. The abuse she suffered from Jonah had been her own private hell.

There was a knock at the door. Michelle was frozen. Darcy motioned for Michelle to leave and go into the kitchen.

"I'm not leaving you alone with that crazy woman. Hasn't she done enough to this family?" Michelle huffed.

"I will be fine. Take the baby and go into the kitchen. I'll call you if I need you."

Michelle swooped down and grabbed A.J. She darted down the hallway to the back of the house. Darcy slowly opened the door. The two women just stared at one another for several seconds. Katie did not seem surprised to see her there. Darcy however, was surprised. She was surprised to see that Katie appeared to be pregnant.

Darcy moved aside, indicating that Katie could come in. Katie dropped her head and entered the house.

"Obviously you never told the police that I was

150

involved in what happened. I don't know why you didn't. Lord knows, I could've stopped it. I'm not here to make excuses for myself or cause problems. I'm here because I have some things to tell you. When I left that day I walked to the shelter about three blocks away. A lady at the shelter talked to me and offered to help me get into a rehab facility. I knew that I was going to end up dead or worse."

Darcy raised her eyebrows with a skeptical look.

"Yes, there is worse Darcy. I've seen it on those streets. I didn't want to be like that. I had to face my demons and that included the things I had done to you and Davis and everyone else in my life. The center got me clean and gave me the money to get back home and rent a place. I'm working in Baxter at a small salon. The woman that owns it is big on giving people second chances, thank God."

"Katie, did you come here to say you're sorry because if you did, don't. I don't expect you to."

"Please just hear me out Darcy. That is only one reason why I'm here. As you can see, I'm pregnant. I'm twenty eight weeks along. They tell me it's a girl." She rubbed her belly as she continued to talk.

"Darcy, this baby belongs to Jonah. I'm sure of it. I haven't been with anyone since the week before I left him and for over a month before that. I can't care for a child. I never wanted kids; Davis will tell you that. I wouldn't be good at it. This child belongs with her family. I'm asking you and Davis to take the baby. She belongs with you two. She's your niece. Yes, I know about you and Jonah being brother and sister. The word gets around in a small town."

Darcy was dumbstruck.

"You can't be serious. I'm sure that you will change your mind once she's born. This is not something you should decide suddenly. If you have straightened out your life you will want to have your daughter with you."

"This decision hasn't been sudden. I've been sure the whole time. I just wanted to give you time to adjust before I dropped in on you. Please think about it and talk with Davis. I'm leaving you my number at work. I don't have a home telephone or a cell. Please give me a call and let me know what you decide."

Katie handed her a small piece of paper with a number written on it. She could see the tears in her eyes as she turned for the door. She paused suddenly, turned, and laid her hand on Darcy's shoulder as she said, "You really are a good person and I hope you can find it in your heart to forgive me."

Katie smiled faintly and walked out the door.

Chapter 46

She would have to tell her soon-to-be husband that his ex-wife wanted them to raise her brother's child. Katie was right. The child deserved to be with her family.

She had to think how this was going to make Michelle feel to see Jonah's daughter every day. It would hurt but Michelle was a good woman. She wouldn't want the child to pay for Jonah's mistakes. This child would be A.J.'s half-sister technically. Darcy ran her fingers through her hair and headed for the kitchen to tell Michelle the news.

That evening when Davis arrived home, Darcy asked to see him upstairs. He playfully swatted her behind and asked, "Wow, can't even wait until after dinner huh?"

"No silly. It isn't that. I have something important to discuss with you. It's serious."

He could tell by the look on her face that it was not your average talk. He sat down on the edge of their king sized bed covered with a brown paisley comforter. She began to explain what happened.

"Have you told Michelle?" Davis asked.

"Yes, and she is in agreement with me. This child is one of us and she deserves a good life."

Davis held his head in his hands for several minutes. This was a big decision. It wasn't as simply as 'what's for supper?'

"Have you told Mom?"

"No. Michelle and I thought it best not to tell her until we make a decision."

The pause just kept lingering. She was wondering if he would ever give her an answer. Finally he looked up and grinned.

"Contact Katie and have her at my office tomorrow afternoon around three. I will have the papers drawn up for a legal adoption. Explain to her that she won't be able to back out of it. This will be our legal daughter from the moment of birth."

Darcy nodded. She couldn't believe that in less than twelve weeks, she would be a mother. She couldn't help but be excited. The next hurdle was to tell Kim. They weren't sure how she would take it. It could go either way. The last thing any of them wanted was to cause Kim any more pain than she had already been through. She took Jonah's death really hard.

The three of them, Darcy, Davis, and Michelle all sat Kim down and told her what would be happening. She fidgeted on the edge of the sofa for a moment and began to cry.

It wasn't tears of sadness. It was tears of joy.

She knew that she would have not one, but two children in her home to remind her of her baby boy. Jonah had made mistakes and Kim knew that but he would always be her baby. She was in total agreement about the child. They began to make arrangements to find a suitable cradle for the new grandchild.

Until the wedding, Darcy and Davis would still be staying at the farm but the urgency to find a house of their own had just increased. The foster children were now down to only two but that still left five other people in the household, not counting the new addition soon to come.

The next day Katie was contacted and the arrangements were made. She showed up at Davis' law office promptly and signed the appropriate papers. Katie had gained weight with the pregnancy. It was becoming to ̴r. The change was good compared to the skinny girl ̾ the disheveled appearance that lived with Jonah. She ̾v thanked him and Darcy for taking her daughter as

̾s a changed person and you could tell it

154

wasn't an act. Time had taught her a lesson that she wouldn't fast forget. As she was leaving the office, she turned to Davis.

"I have never done one unselfish thing in my life. This will be the first and it feels good."

Relief flooded Davis. He had spent the night getting his hopes up. The idea of taking his brother's child and raising her had tugged at his heart strings. He wanted to do right by her and give her a good life just like he was trying to help Michelle do with A.J. It was early that morning when he thought Katie might back out of the offer. He knew that they would all be crushed if she didn't show up. But she did! She showed up right on time and held up her end of the bargain. Darcy looked radiant as Katie closed the door on her way out.

"Well, I guess we have ourselves a daughter. Are you as excited as I am?" Darcy asked.

"Yes honey. I am very happy. My concern now is to keep an eye on Katie to make sure that she continues to want to do the right thing. We can't risk her slipping into drugs again while she's carrying our child."

That had never crossed Darcy's mind before. Fear shot through her for a moment and suddenly a peace took over and she knew that it would be okay. Their daughter would be just fine.

Chapter 47

The holidays passed swiftly. Between the wedding plans and Katie's doctor appointments, Darcy was very busy. Katie was doing beautifully. She was working hard and sticking with her substance abuse classes. She was even eating healthy for the baby's sake. Davis had never seen her so dedicated to anything. She continually promised him and Darcy that she was taking good care of their child.

They went to every appointment with Katie and things were progressing just fine. They were able to see the ultrasound and actually got to look at the baby. Darcy was amazed. She felt almost envious of Davis' ex-wife. It must be a great feeling to have life growing inside of you. She knew she was being a little petty. Her time would come and she would have many children that she could carry in her womb.

Lying in bed that night Darcy told Davis, "I've thought of a name. I think we should name her Kimberly Michelle, after her grandmother and her aunt. We could call her Shelly. What do you think?"

"I think that's a wonderful name. Shelly Boyden it is."

The furnishings were ready and the house was stocked for a new baby. Everyone was on pins and needles. February was in full swing and Katie's due date was fast approaching. Darcy had gone into town with Kim to get groceries when her cell phone began ringing.

"Hello?"

"Miss Scott, this is Dr. Wolton. I'm at the hospital Katie Boyden and she is in active labor. She's ˙ to eight centimeters and completely effaced. I should get here as soon as possible. This looks ˙g to be a swift delivery."

This was it. The time had come!

Darcy called Davis as Kim turned the car toward the hospital. Both cars were pulling in at the same time. They all rushed up to the maternity ward. Nurses were waiting to suit them up.

The once cozy room with the rocking chair had been transformed into a major medical arena. Nurses we scattered everywhere. Some were checking machines hooked to Katie; others were asking her questions or giving her instructions. Darcy was overwhelmed.

"You two the parents I suppose?" a large female nurse asked. Her name tag said Mary but she looked more like a Bertha. I would hate to tangle with her, Davis thought.

"Yes we are," Darcy answered.

"Good. She's been asking for you both this whole time. You better get over here. It won't be long now."

Mary (Bertha) led the three of them to Katie's bedside. She was drenched in sweat and obviously in a lot of pain. Darcy took her hand.

"Oh Lord! This hurts so badly! I'm glad you guys got here so fast. They say that I'm doing good but it sure feels like I'm dying."

Katie's breathing was rapid and strained. She was trying so hard to be strong.

"You're doing great. Just hang in there and it will be over before you know it," Darcy coached.

"Easy…for…you…to…say…you…haven't… had…," Katie began to trail off.

Suddenly her eyes rolled back in her head. A nurse shouted, "BP bottoming out! We're losing the baby's heart rate and the mother's too!"

Darcy felt sick like she could vomit any minute. What was going on? What happened to 'she's doing so good?' Please God don't let anything happen to our baby, she silently prayed.

"You all have to go out of the room. She's bleeding internally. We're going to have to rush her into a emergency cesarean. We'll come get you when we know something."

That was all the doctor said to them before he pushed them into the hallway. They were told to wait.

What a horrible word, wait. It seemed the hardest thing to do when you are waiting on something you wanted so badly. Kim lead them down to the chapel and the three of them sat together waiting for the words that could make or break them.

Darcy called Michelle. She had gotten home from picking up A.J.

Michelle had gone back to school to become a therapist. She said she thought she would be good at it and it would give her a chance to build a new life for herself and her son. She was currently attending school and leaving the baby with a sitter during the day. Michelle told her to call as soon as they knew any information.

It was close to an hour before the doctor came to the chapel wearing his green scrubs. Everyone in the room braced themselves for the worst but hoped for the best.

"Ms. Boyden was bleeding out. She had a problem with her uterus that we couldn't see during her exams. When labor began, it caused her to hemorrhage. We had to do a full hysterectomy on her but she will be fine. The baby was delivered in time to avoid any problems. She is healthy and weighs seven pounds and two ounces. Would you like to see her now?"

Each one felt the weight of the world come off their shoulders.

"Yes, we would," Davis said.

Everyone jumped up to follow the doctor down the 'lway. He led them into a different wing and up to the 'ow. She was in the first row by the front. You could little pink and white tag that said "Baby Boyden". 'orgeous. Her hair was a mop of dark black just 'r. The only resemblance to Katie that Darcy could see was the little turned up nose. No one would ever be able to see that this child had belonged to anyone but her and her husband.

"Has Katie seen her?" Darcy asked.

"No, we don't bring the baby to the birth mother when the sealed adoption has already taken place," Dr. Wolton answered.

"May I take her to see Katie?" she asked.

"Darcy, do you think that's a good idea?" Davis replied.

She nodded yes. The nurse behind the glass bundled up little Shelly Boyden and brought her out to her new mommy. After Daddy and Grandma got to hold her she set off for Katie's room.

Chapter 48

The door creaked open and Katie turned to look. Darcy was standing in the doorway holding the baby. She wasn't sure if she wanted to see her or not. It might be too hard.

"May we come in?"

"Sure."

"I wanted you to see your daughter. If you don't want to, I'll respect that and go away but you had your say when you came to our house to offer her to us. Now, I want to have my say."

Katie held out her hand for Darcy and the baby to sit on the edge of her bed.

"When Jonah had me kidnapped, you were the only one who showed me any compassion. I knew in my heart that you didn't want to hurt me. I saw it. I also know that the things you have lived through have hurt you and you're trying to start over. I just want you to go away from this knowing how very much we thank you for this child. We will care for her and raise her with every ounce of love she could ever hope for. You are a good person Katie."

For a moment Katie's words hung in her throat.

"Thank you for that. I don't feel good sometimes but I'm trying really hard. I should feel upset that they had to do a hysterectomy on me since you are taking the baby but I don't. I know that this happened for a reason and I'm fine with it. You tell her one day when she's old enough about me and let her know I gave her away because I loved her. Please."

Darcy smiled. "I will indeed. Thank you again."

'ith that last goodbye Darcy was out the door and 'he thought it was best that they not have any more 'ith Katie. The job was done. The purpose was '' was time to move into the future.

Epilogue

Davis and Darcy wed in the spring of that year with all their family and friends cheering them on. The following year Michelle found a nice man who had asked her to marry him. He was very accepting of the Boyden family and was good to A.J. The child had no memory of his father. That was probably for the best. Jonah's son never needed to know the dark history of his father's last days. He would be loved by a mother and a father in a happy home. A.J. deserved that.

Davis had purchased a home not far from the ranch so that they could bring Shelly to see her grandmother often. Being parents had only made them closer. It made Darcy's heart full to see Kim dote on her daughter. There was nothing that could make her any happier, or so she thought.

When Shelly was eighteen months old, Darcy found out she was pregnant. It had finally happened. All she had ever hoped for had come to her. She would be able to see her children grow up with the love she had only for a short time. Her babies would be surrounded with the loving family she always wanted. Marco was even a constant fixture in their home. He missed his chance to be a father to his son and daughter but he wasn't missing his chance to be a grandfather.

Watching Shelly climb on that old rope bridge and feeling the life inside her tummy made Darcy realize that the journey across the bridge of life may be hard at times, but if you hang on, don't give up and make it to the other side, you might just find everything you're looking for.